**RED** ... **SURE**

*For my son Louis "Baba Yaga"*

# Contents

# CHAPTER 1

Jacob Rivers was an art dealer. When he was not attending galleries or exhibitions, he could be found in his shop framing pictures and creating his own works. The name of the shop was 'Knightsbridge', and it was located on King Street, City Centre Manchester surrounded by high end boutiques, jewellers, tailors and bars. It was a bright, clean and contemporary space with a few well-chosen designs and paintings adorning the wall space. With a two-sided cushioned bench in the centre, it had the feel of a spacious miniature gallery, allowing customer's room to browse in a relaxed atmosphere. At the back there was a room he used for framing, a small meticulously kept office and next to that, a door leading to a basement.

When he had finished for the day, Jacob checked the CCTV was working correctly before putting on his suit jacket. He turned off the lights and walked through the shop floor to the front door. Satisfied that the alarm was set, Jacob locked the door behind him and placed the keys back in his pocket. Turning to look both ways, he set off down the street.

Jacob liked to dress well. He particularly loved the feel of a suit and the way, that despite it supposedly being designed to make a statement, it could also allow a person in a city to easily blend into the background as just another suit in the busy city. He occasionally found the need to dodge the odd person walking towards him on the crowded street, either oblivious to his existence or, as he sometimes felt, purposely trying to collide with him to prove some sort of point. He was just under 6ft and slight of build, so did not have an imposing stature, but he still kept alert and resisted making eye contact so not to invite any unwanted attention.

He felt the wind pick up and catch his tie and suit jacket as he turned towards King Street West open-air car park. It was a breezy but dry Tuesday afternoon in late July, which made a change from the weeks of rain which had recently fallen over the city.

As he approached his car, he pressed the key fob and unlocked it with a beep and a flash. It was a black Land Rover Defender; a car like this certainly helped when collecting or moving paintings but it also helped that he liked the look of them. Strong and stylish. Climbing into the driver's seat, his phone gave a message alert. He glanced at the screen - it was an email from someone called Laura Appleton with the subject "framing photos for exhibition". One to read back at home, he thought as he started the car, put it in gear, and pulled away.

•••

It had been a few days since Laura Appleton received the phone call from Jean Willis at Maxus Imagery. They had seen some of her work online and were keen to use some of it at an upcoming event. For a while Laura had been covering events to maintain her income but her passion and talent truly lay in portrait photography. Over the years she had amassed an impressive portfolio, highlights of which she hosted on her website and social media - one of the places where Jean herself had seen her work.

The kettle clicked off and the sound of boiling water woke Laura from her reverie. Pushing her glasses further up her nose and pulling her hair behind her ears, she rose from the work bench and made coffee, not once looking away from the laptop screen. She was sure of all the work she had done these were the six images she would have framed for the Maxus imagery event. Laura wanted to make the best impression, however, and needed the images framed well. A search of local businesses online, lead her to a website that had just what she was looking for, Knightsbridge. Laura clicked the contact tab and began typing. As she did so she felt a rush of excitement. It was real, it was happening.

•••

Jacob pulled into the driveway fifty minutes after setting off. His house was located in Wilmslow and it reflected his style and success. It had a white limestone lower and dark wood upper facade with large windows and a garage. The ground floor was open plan, with a dining area to the left and a kitchen with breakfast bar at the back. To the right was a staircase, a utility room and lounge area. Upstairs were two large bedrooms with walk-in wardrobes and en-suite facilities, and a spacious study. Once inside he closed the door and gently hung his keys on the key hook. As he entered the room, he looked around and noted everything exactly as it should be. He stopped after a few steps and listened, silence. Satisfied, he sat at the kitchen bench and took out his phone.

Two messages, the first Laura Appleton: "Good afternoon, I am due to exhibit some photography in a few weeks. I wondered if we might be able to discuss framing of six prints. Kind regards, Laura."

Second message anonymous sender: "There's a fly problem which could use pest control".

It is going to be a busy week he thought and moved to his laptop. Logging on to the secure server, a black screen with a single folder named flies. In the folder was a single document containing images and brief description:

Job reference: 634
Name: Gregory John Malcolm. Year of birth 1962, Height: 6ft 2".

Jacob could see that from the picture Gregory was badly overweight, bald with thick eyebrows, dark beard and a crooked nose. He also had large tribal tattoos covering his arms and a neck tattoo of "XXX". A distinctive fellow who would be noticeable in any scenario. He continued to read:

Contract: Exclusive.
Method: Open. Vehicle: Bentley Continental, private License number GJM.
Offenses: Assault & battery leading to fatality, domestic abuse, Intimidation, soliciting prostitution, Supply and distribution of narcotics. All verified.
Expiration date: At earliest convenience
Location: Domestic. Manchester
Remuneration: 80k
 Accept- reply 5 / Reject- reply 8.

Jacob committed the information to memory and logged off from the server. To anonymous he replied by text with nothing more than the number 5 and deleted the message from his phone. He then replied to Laura.

•••

Fatigue began to set in. It was a small gym located around the corner from her flat and Laura had been on the tread mill at high pace for over an hour. She slowed the machine to a brisk walk and breathed deeply, sweat beading across her forehead. She had always been active and took pride in being in good shape - years of yoga and running had rewarded her with a toned physique. After five minutes warming down, she ended the machine's program. She wiped her face with a towel and made her way to the changing room where she showered and dressed. On her way out she checked her phone to see one new message. "Laura! Congratulations on your exhibition. I would be more than happy to discuss your framing requirements. Please pop into the shop anytime between nine and four Monday to Friday. It may help if you bring some examples to see they sit in each frame. Kind regards, Jacob."

A small smile crept across Laura's lips, the thought of the exhibit in a few weeks and all the preparation required beforehand filled her with excitement. 'Tomorrow is as good a time as any' she thought, not one to waste time or put things off. Finding a renewed rush of energy, she started across the gym car park making her way home.

Wednesday 04:30am, the alarm clock sounded. Jacob reached an arm over to the bed side table to silence it. He rose slowly, rotating his shoulders and neck beginning his morning routine. At forty years old he had managed to keep his body in remarkable condition. At ten per percent body fat, he was lean and athletic. His routine was engineered around strength and stamina more than muscle gain. He began with half an hour of stretches. After this he began his calisthenics and ended with twenty minutes of yoga. Coated in a fine sweat with his heart slightly elevated he took a lukewarm shower. The cool water sharpened his focus.

After ten minutes he was towelled off and selecting his clothes for the day. A three-piece navy-blue suit with a white shirt and steel grey wool knit tie. He fixed his hair in the mirror and noted the few grey hairs appearing in the stubble that covered his face and a few more lines around the eyes. "I could definitely use a holiday after this next job" he thought. "Somewhere with good art; culture, good wine and agreeable temperature". Pulling himself back to the present, he gave himself an assured nod in the mirror, turned and left the bedroom to begin the day.

•••

In his hotel room Gregory Malcolm opened his eyes and swiftly recognized the consequences of excess. His head hurt. His eyes struggled to focus. It must have been three or four in the morning when he had finally passed out. He turned his head to find in the bed next to him lay the naked torso of a prostitute he did not remember staying. He was also naked too, and he stank. He placed his thumb and index finger to the corner of his eyes and exhaled loudly. Regret was not something that haunted Gregory, even as a child torturing insects, abusing animals or beating up classmates - even punching his own mother was not something that caused a shameful second thought. In his world Gregory was King. He made his money by flooding cities with narcotics. He recruited runners and peddlers to corrupt and ruin what would otherwise have been better lives, enslaving users of all backgrounds into a limited life of misery and dependence. It paid remarkably well.

Gregory swung his legs off the bed. His head pounded as the blood shifted from gravity. A brief wave of nausea passed over him and his eyes refocused. He looked down at his hairy chest and protruding belly. He scratched his testicles and felt a sticky residue coat his fingers. Raising his hand to his nose and sniffing, his stomach churned. "Dirty fucking bitch!" he said in a harsh Liverpudlian accent to the unconscious brunette and wondered what the possibilities were that he had caught another STD - not once giving any regard as to what he may have passed on to his unwitting companion.
Gregory showered, the heat causing him to throw up the remnant of last night's Champagne from his stomach. A mix of suds and bile swirled around his feet before spinning round the plug hole. When finished he wrapped a towel around his waist, draped another over his hairy shoulders and retrieved his phone from the tracksuit pants crumpled on the floor by the bed. He searched his contacts, found Terry and pressed call. As it rang, he stared at the sleeping

stranger, and felt anger rising in him. On the third ring a voice answered. "Hey Terry, I need to speak to Charlie, they didn't show with the shit last night, waste of my fucking time..."

After a brief pause Terry coldly replied "You were over an hour late to the deal, spotters saw you rock up playing the big shot, drunk out your skull with a car full of women. The deal went south, it was your fault and Charlie knows. This is strike two Greg, you're slipping and we can't afford baggage." Gregory hated being spoken down to, he felt his jaw clench, "Look, I'll speak to them and sort it, tell Charlie I'll sort it okay?" After another pause Terry spoke "last chance, get it done before the new business in Salford, and for your sake, don't screw it up". With that the call ended.

Gregory dressed himself in his creased Blue EA7 Armani tracksuit. He sank down on to the edge of the bed to pull on his Adidas trainers, the force on the springs waking the young woman. She turned to face Gregory "where's my money?" she mumbled. Gregory stood and grimaced as he looked her over. "You should be paying me" he said, "You had the time of your life." He made a start toward the door. The young woman sprung to her feet, approached him and in a raised voice she said, "For what I had to put up with you better have my money!" Less than a meter apart Gregory cupped the young lady's face with his hand, "Shhh, it's ok" he said, "no need for this to get out of hand, eh?" With a swift hook of his right arm his fist connected with her jaw knocking her unconscious instantly. Legs giving way she collapsed in a naked heap to the floor. With that Gregory turned and left, he had things to do.

•••

Thursday 10:45am, Laura walked slowly through the bustling city street. It was a warm day with barely any clouds. Under the trees, sunlight cast shadows on the pavement as the gentle breeze made the leaves dance. She carried her portfolio on her shoulder with the prints she'd chosen for display in it. Gathering her bearings, she headed towards King Street to find Knightsbridge. She noted the varying boutiques as she made her way through the crowds on the pavement. A little way ahead she saw a modern looking shop front. It was well maintained white with two large windows. Between them two steps led to the door, above which a sign read Knightsbridge. As she entered the shop a bell rang overhead. She looked around. There was one other customer browsing the hanging artwork. He was a tall thin black man with a pencil style moustache, a black fedora hat and he was dressed in a light grey checked three-piece suit, with black loafers without socks. The photographer in her couldn't help but think of how she would capture his image. Next, she noticed how each of the images on display had been given its own space. None of them were crowded. It was quality over quantity, each piece could breathe. She liked that. It showed the owner was interested in the art on show and was keen to show it in its best light. Laura almost felt as though she were at an exhibition. She scanned the works on offer by, Rozanne Bell, Keith McBride, Simon Wright, and Paul Oz.   As she studied a photography piece, she heard the gentleman speak as a figure emerged from somewhere behind the viewing area holding a painting. "Oh, how marvellous, yes! Yes! This is exactly what I was looking for, Jacob my dear. However, did you manage to get your hands on one?" Laura glanced over but could only see the back of the painting, the customer looked pleased with whatever was presented to him. To the left of the customer was the man referred to as Jacob, in a well fitted dark blue suit. Neat but styled salt and pepper hair. He appeared calm and assured and well kept. He was handsome with a slightly olive skin tone. Slim but toned. Not particularly tall but not short either. He had a days' worth of stubble which suited his features. He had cold blue eyes. Just then, he looked up and caught Laura assessing him and smiled. Not a big smile, more of a welcoming and inclusive smile as though they were all sharing the moment. Laura glanced away, wondering why she felt as though she had been caught somewhere she shouldn't have been. She realized she was also holding her breath and exhaled. He must be the owner she thought and continued browsing until the jolly customer was done.

"What did we agree on, twenty-five? More than happy.  You have the details?" Jacob nodded "Great then I'll take it now, thanks again handsome you've made my year, see you again." And with that the man with the fedora made his way out the door arms wide holding the A3 size painting which was now encased in a protective covering.
She had been stood looking at the same picture for about five minutes. It was a painting on canvas of a couple at a train station with two suitcases. The couple were sharing a loving embrace as if reunited after time apart. Jacob watched her for a moment

before approaching. "That one is by Richard Blunt called Always back to you" He said. Laura turned towards him.

"Oh yes, I like this - the use of light and contrast is wonderful". He detected a London accent.

"Jacob Rivers. Nice to meet you" he said introducing himself with a slight bow and his hands clasped behind his back.

"Ah, Laura, Laura Appleton, I emailed you about some frames." Said Laura as she moved her hair behind her ears.

"Yes Laura of course. The photographer with the upcoming exhibit. I take it that's your portfolio for the showing?" He said gesturing to the bag on Laura's shoulder.

"Yes, this is my work. I would like to frame them with something that complements the tones".

"Of course, shall we?" Jacob said, gesturing to the back of the shop. "Please follow me."

"These are remarkable." Jacob said, looking at the photographs. "The story, the tones...Where is the exhibition?" He asked.

"It's with Maxus Imagery, in a few weeks, it's being held at Starlight Gallery. Do you know it?" Laura asked.

"Yes, I know it, as it happens, I'll be attending to hopefully buy some works. Maxus is a good broker; you must be incredibly pleased to have been asked. I mean it's only fitting though; your work is...." Jacob was so enthralled he trailed off. Laura turned her gaze from the image to Jacob. She found herself enjoying the wonder in his expression as he looked at her work.

"Ok" he said turning on his heels - the movement so fluid it caught Laura off guard. "Let me get... ah here" he said as he shifted through a stack of frame samples. After a minute he returned to the bench and laid down three. Holding the first over the image he said "now this one is subtle, straight lines. Minimalist. Darker charcoal perimeter, lighter almost metallic inner to help draw the eye and works well with the tones, the contrast and light, particularly for the light of the venue". He looked at Laura to gauge any kind of response. "This is nice, yes. Not too bold but becomes and enhancement of the image". She smiled. He began Selecting a different image and overlaying a different frame. There was something about him Laura could not quite figure out. He had a commanding yet relaxing presence. He was one to take charge of the situation. Her curiosity piqued, "So you're going to the event?" asked Laura.

•••

In the dark sub-basement of the central car park, Gregory was passing "spice" out to his two runners. Spice has plagued many people, particularly the city's growing homeless population. It is a laboratory-made drug that mimics the effect of the main psychoactive component of cannabis. Often rendering the user in a catatonic state.

"You make sure you get the full amount, even if the bastards start begging. Yous get that money or I will fuckin' do you both in!" Gregory spat out the window.

From what could be seen of their faces under their hoodies and caps, the two runners looked like zombies - gaunt, drawn and pale. Eyes hollow in their sockets. They took their wares, turned, and shuffled off. Like mindless drones. It was easy to control people when you had the very thing they were addicted too. Fear of being cut off kept broken dogs obedient.

He dialled the contact in his phone with no name. He had messed up the deal Charlie and Terry had set up to start supplying ketamine and had to make it right. He knew he would have to offer some collateral for showing up late, so had sent his runners out to double their efforts. If collateral were going to be paid, the spaced-out street rats would pay for it he thought. The phone rang; it was answered on the fourth ring.

"Who's this?" Gregory was startled to hear a female voice. She had a European accent he couldn't place.

"Err, this is Greg, from the erm, mobile pharmacy, look, I wanted to say sorry and all that for the other day, erm, how about we rearrange it, get my boss off my back like?" There was an uncomfortable pause, Gregory shifted in his seat. Leather creaked.

"The terms have changed, 2k more on each load. We can meet same place and time tonight, trade."

Even with his runners doing their best he knew he would be short with the new deal. He could either try charming her or negotiate a better price, or else he would have to stump the money up himself which he certainly did not want to do. However, he knew the deal had to go ahead or he would be in the firing line and in this business that was quite literal. It would be a death sentence. "Listen darling" he began, "that's a lot of money, you're asking for ten bricks like it's just lying around!"

There was another pause before she answered, "there is no discussion, you agree, or we talk to others".

"Fine, bring the shit and we'll get it done." He hung up. "Fucking bitch!" He shouted. His face turned red with anger. This meant he had to front the money for his mistake.

•••

Between the few browsing customers, in little over an hour, Laura and Jacob had finalized the frames for the six pieces. The aspects of light, tone and contrast of the photography as well as the venue and its lighting had been considered. In all, every aspect had been discussed to present each piece at its best. "So, when do you think they'll be done?" asked Laura, her gaze remaining on the work before them until she had finished asking the question. He looked at her, for a moment Laura was not sure if she should look away. She kept eye contact, her mouth opening a little. He noticed how blue her eyes were.

"I can have them ready by next week" said Jacob smiling.

"Great" said Laura you have no idea how worried I was, this whole thing has caught me completely by surprise."

"Don't worry" said Jacob, "it will be fine. Who are you taking for support on the big night?" His question threw her. She had not considered the thought of taking someone. In fact, she had not long been in Manchester.

"Um, well, I've recently moved here, well three months now and I've not had a chance to speak to anyone back home yet, as I say bit of a shock. It's only really me and Mum."

"Well, you can either come back to the shop to collect these" he said, "or I can deliver them to the exhibit.

I'll be attending anyway so if you're stuck for company there's always me." Although he meant it as a friendly gesture, he caught himself. True he was going to be there, yes, he would no doubt see her there but there was something else, a desire to see her, spend time with her again. He wanted to know more about her. This would not do - this was a distraction he could not afford. She smiled at him. She had a warm, pretty smile.

"Right" he said, "so will you be collecting, or shall I deliver them to the venue?"

"Oh, the venue please, I don't have a car". She replied.

"Very well" he said, in the meantime, you know where I am and.... here's a business card, call me if you need to, for anything". "What am I doing?" he thought this was something he had never dealt with before -it was as if he was not in control of himself. Against his better judgement he was captivated. He found her utterly fascinating.

•••

8:45pm, lower central car park. Gregory sat in his Bentley Continental smoking a cigarette. Next to him sat Pauli, one of his crew. "These lads coming or what?" asked Pauli irritably.

"Probably late to prove some sort of point, think they're King like. Spoke to some proper stupid bitch earlier...what's this, must be them now kid".

Gregory and Pauli watched as a Mercedes 4x4 crept towards them and then pulled into a spot, leaving two spaces between them and Gregory's car. The rear window rolled down and a stern looking man peered at them. In a European accent he said, "good to see you didn't get lost this time".

Gregory and Pauli looked at each other not appreciating the comment. Gregory reached into the glove box and took out the Sig Sauer P-225 handgun. Getting out of the car, cigarette hanging from his lips; he turned his back to the Mercedes and tucked it into his waist band. Pauli also got out and stood leaning against the side of Gregory's car. Two stocky men stepped out of the Mercedes in unison, the driver staying inside. They looked ex-military and wore serious looks.

"Alright lads? How we doing eh? We all good yeah?" asked Gregory walking round to the two men.

"You have the full amount, yes?" Asked the first man with grey hair.

"Pauli, grab the money" ordered Gregory. Pauli Leaned through the window and grabbed the bag off the passenger seat. "All there lads! What you got for me then eh?" asked Gregory continuing to approach the men rubbing his hands together. The second of the two severe looking men pulled a holdall from the rear seat of the Mercedes and threw it on the floor.

"Check it, we will check the payment". said the man with grey hair holding his hand out to Pauli to signify he wanted the bag. Pauli looked to Gregory who nodded consent. Walking slowly Pauli handed the bag over. The grey-haired man took the bag to the back seat of the car and checked it over. Satisfied he confirmed with his colleagues in Czech "jeho vše tady jde!" and they began to leave.

"Woah, just a fucking minute!" shouted Gregory walking faster his hand reaching for the gun in his waistband.

Pauli made towards the Mercedes as it began to reverse not entirely sure what he would do when he got there. From the rear window the grey-haired man said, you have what you need little bitch!" Gregory and Pauli stopped in their tracks as the Mercedes pulled away. Bending down to open the bag Gregory opened it and looked inside. True to their word it was all there. "Thank fuck for that!" Gregory said to Pauli. Rubbing his hands together, "let's make some fucking money eh?"

•••

Back in his home, Jacob was in his lounge. With his phone to his ear.   After a few rings a lady's voice answered, "Extension please?" she said.

"0502" Jacob replied.

"Control?" she asked.

"Rainbow" he said.

"And confirm caller ID?"

"Grey Wolf"."

"One moment sir, putting you through."

Jacob sat back in his chair and crossed one leg over the other.

"Grey Wolf, I hope you are well, what is your query?" asked the control known as Rainbow.

He had been Jacob's control for over five years now. Providing work and Intelligence to help agents such as Jacob complete assignments and earning commission upon successful completion. Much like a recruitment consultant, his job was finding the right candidate for the task. "Intel please, including locations for one Gregory John Malcolm, Job reference 634," said Jacob.

After a pause Rainbow replied "Most work interactions carried out at central parking, lower level. The mark is known to carry a firearm - pistol usually. Frequents China White, Deansgate on weekends. On Friday's he makes a weekend drop before indulging, usually around 8pm."

"That's received, punching in" Jacob said, confirming the information was understood and that he planned to act soon.

"Card punched, goodbye" said Rainbow and with that the call ended. It was Thursday evening so tomorrow would be the night.

•••

Laura had spent the best part of the evening updating her website in preparation for the event. Satisfied all was in order, she checked her calendar for the following day - she had one customer for some promotional work in the morning. Her studio was in her main living space in her one-bedroom city centre flat. She had been in Manchester for three months now and so far, things were going well. She had been born and raised in Chiswick, London but wanted branch out and make it on her own and, besides, there was enough competition in London. She stood on the balcony and looked out, watching the people below wandering back and forth for a while. She had to admit that at times she was lonely having left her mother and friends behind, but her work was important to her and she felt the need to follow her instincts. Going back inside, she poured herself a glass of wine and sat on the couch. "Jacob Rivers" she said aloud before taking a sip. Opening her laptop again, she then took to the internet to find out what she could about him.

•••

Friday was wet and overcast. Jacob had his sleeves rolled up and wore a dark blue joiner's apron to protect his clothing. He was busy making the frames for Laura's prints and hoped to have the woodwork for all six completed by the end of the day, so he could begin treatment the following week. He had always loved working with his hands, particularly with wood. He found all the processes calming; from cutting, lathe work, chiselling, sanding, priming and painting. Each frame painstakingly created with as much attention and care and as a painter or sculptor creating their latest masterpiece. Often overlooked, a frame could either support a piece of work or, if it were the wrong colour or type it had the potential to tarnish an otherwise beautiful piece. While he worked in the studio area, he locked the shop door and customers could gain access by using the intercom. Due to the rain not, many had required admittance today. There was an older gent looking for a gift for his wife and a young university art student looking at work and asking questions, which Jacob was only too happy to help. It was a productive day. Perfect as the evening has the potential to be quite volatile. Not that he was fazed by the prospect. Jacob was quite adept at protecting himself should the need arise.

Growing up he became quite accomplished in judo and boxing; however, he found his niche with the fighting style known as Defendu. Defendu, or "Gutter fighting", was a hand-to-hand combat system originally developed by William E. Fairbairn around 1926. It was taught to British and allied troops in World War 2. In its military application, and in modern terms, it's more commonly known as close quarter combat. Defendu encourages its practitioner to end a confrontation as quickly as possible using "ungentlemanly" means by rapidly attacking vital areas such as the groin, throat and side of the neck, shin, eyes, or ears. Despite his appearance as a slim, unthreatening art dealer, with his experience, knowledge and access to weaponry Jacob could be considered highly dangerous. Still, it paid to be grounded, many of his colleagues who took on similar assignments had met an untimely end or imprisonment when a job went bad, despite meticulous planning. This line of work was high risk, much more so than the art world, but it had its benefits. Not just the financial incentive but also the satisfaction of serving the community when failed by the justice system.

Targets were submitted to the Committee by various people, usually by a victim represented by a member of the law enforcement agency because for some reason or another, justice was not served. Before a case can become active, targets are subjected to the equivalent of background checks to ensure that they meet the criteria. Once approved the nominee backs the application with a non-refundable bounty priced by the committee. Not just anyone could be a target of course, there was a strict screening process; No political or religious targets for personal gain. The committee would only accept targets based on criminal cause and would not entertain petty revenge requests against exes or bosses no matter what the bounty. The aim is to make the world a better place by ridding it of evil, verified evil not glorified murder for profit like in Hollywood films. It was complicated but the aim was to serve the ultimate justice when justice failed. In this case, someone had quite enough of the exploits of one Gregory Malcolm and agreed to front £80,000 to ensure his eradication from this world.

19:12, finished with the frames, Jacob carried out the usual checks before closing the shop, however this time instead of going home, he unlocked the basement door, pulled the light cord hanging inside the door and walked down the wooden stairs to open plan area below. It was a perfectly rectangular room, painted white. Like everything in Jacob's life, it was neat and well ordered. There were cabinets around the walls and a table in the centre. On one wall there was a large city map, on the wall opposite there was a chest with a numerical padlock. He knelt by the chest being careful not to put his knee in the floor, so as not to spoil his suit. Rotating the numbers, he heard a distinctive click and the lock sprung open. From inside he retrieved two small objects both wrapped in black cloth and carried them to the where he carefully unwrapped them. The first contained a Glock 17 handgun which had a 17 x 9mm round capacity. The second contained a selection of tactical knives. He selected one and strapped it to his right ankle He removed his suit jacket and pulled on a shoulder holster from the chest and he inserted a magazine before holstering the gun. As he carefully put his jacket back on, he peered into the chest. The last thing he took out were a pair of black leather gloves. As was now tradition, he stood for a few minutes planning his approach, visualizing his actions. Over the course on ten years, this would be his nineteenth assignment. He was starting to consider stopping at his twentieth. He had carried out his service; he owned his shop, house, cars and had enough to retire very comfortably. Best quit while ahead he thought. He breathed deeply. It was almost time. He focussed his mind once again on the target, Gregory Malcolm; assault, one which led to a fatality, drugs and intimidation. With that he walked purposefully back up the stairs, turned off the light and locked the door.

As usual, at 8:00pm on a Friday night, Gregory was in the sub-basement of the central car park. One by one, half-starved junkie runners paid him a visit for their weekly one to ones and to collect their merchandise for the weekend. As he was talking to one of his 'employees', Gregory noticed a man in a suit, holding his stomach and staggering as he made his way toward them. "Look at this fucking piss head eh?" He said. The runner laughed in agreement. "I want the lot gone; do you understand? Start in the Northern quarter and get them students, easy money" he ordered. The runner nodded and shuffled off.

The office worker staggered closer. Gregory pulled a joint from his cigarette box, lit it and took a deep drag. "Look at the fucking state of you!" he shouted. The drunken man was within a few meters of the car now, walking unsteadily with his head down. "Are you driving home, eh dick head?"

The office worker fell over, crashing into the rear of Gregory's car. "The fuck you doing?" Gregory shouted opening the door and springing out. He rushed towards the crouched man and grabbed him by the shoulder. Quick as a flash, Jacob swung round

180 degrees, left arm up to protect his head and his right fist connecting with Gregory's Addams Apple. His right elbow followed to the face knocking the joint from Gregory's lips before an upward palm strike to the jaw, snapped Gregory's head back. Jacob carried through with the momentum forcing Gregory off balance until he fell backwards. There was a high-pitched sound ringing in Gregory's ears as his head smacked against the tarmac. While he lay dazed, Jacob seized the opportunity and gained a mounted position administering a barrage of heavy palm, elbow and fist strikes to his targets face. Within ten seconds Gregory lay on the car park floor semi-conscious, his face a bloody pulp. Jacob reached two gloved hands forward and gripped tightly around his neck. Gregory's eyes bulged, his arms now too weak and his brain too shaken to defend himself. His legs kicked out under Jacob in a futile attempt. Terror showing in his eyes while his vision faded to black. After a few minutes of pathetic resistance, Gregory's influence on the world was gone. Jacob stood slowly checking for any witnesses. All was quiet. He dragged the lifeless body to the rear of the car, opened the boot and heaved Gregory up, tipping him inside. Smoothing down his clothes, Jacob pushed the boot door closed and calmly settled himself into the driver's seat. With the keys still in the ignition, Jacob started the engine and exited the car park. Job half done; it was time to dispose of the remnants.

•••

In a disused industrial area on the outskirts of the city, the flames of a burning Bentley lit up the night sky with Gregory being cremated in the boot. No doubt the police will eventually find the charred shell of the car and whatever remained of the body but, anything that could tie Jacob to the incident would be long gone. Jacob took a slow walk back to the city to collect his car and return home. He was looking forward to a shower and glass or two of red wine. He called Rainbow and confirmed the contract had been completed. Since he needed no materials or weaponry once Rainbow takes his commission, Jacob will claim £60,000. Not bad for a couple of hours work.

As he began his journey back into the city his phone rang with a number he didn't recognise. "Knightsbridge" he said. "H-hello? um it's Laura here, we met earlier, is this Jacob?" Her voice was nervous, perhaps tipsy. "Yes, this is Jacob. Laura what a pleasant surprise, is there something I can help you with?" He said. "I'm fine I just, well, I wondered..." she trailed off. "You wondered?" repeated Jacob. Laura sat in her couch put her hand to her head and closed her eyes and said "I wondered if you weren't busy tomorrow, tomorrow night, then maybe we could meet for a drink? To discuss art of course "Jacob felt a smile spread across his face "that would be great, would you like to have dinner as well?" Laura could feel herself blushing "that sounds great shall we meet at erm, I don't know, maybe at St Ann's square at seven?" She asked. "Seven it is, I look forward to it". "Seven then" she repeated, "seven" Jacob confirmed. "Great, ok then good night" Laura said, "goodnight Laura" said Jacob as they ended the call. It was a few miles back to the car park, but he smiled the entire way.

# CHAPTER 2

6:50PM Laura stood nervously in St Ann's square near the steps which led to the Theatre. The square was well lit and offered high end shops, bars and cafes. Trees and monuments ran down the centre of the square and St Ann's church to the south of the square. She scrolled through her social media feed while she waited, occasionally looking up to see if she could see Jacob approaching. She had been there for fifteen minutes. Even knowing she was early she was filled with dread that she might be stood up. Jacob had seen her arrive. He did not want to appear too eager, so he decided to observe from a distance just for a moment. He was trying to catch something, understand something about her in that moment but he did not quite know what. For the first time in a long time, he felt under prepared. He didn't do this sort of thing, but he found himself drawn to her -he couldn't explain it. He surveyed the square once more, drew a deep breath and began to approach her.

Laura scanned the square and saw Jacob walking towards her, smiling. "Hi, I wasn't sure if you were going to come. I am so sorry for the call last night. It had been a hard week. I was a mess and things…." She realized she was on auto ramble. He listened, genuinely enthralled. "It was great to hear from you" he said. Taking her hands from her coat pocket she made a motion, but she was not entirely sure what to do, she made an awkward attempt of something between a hug and a handshake. Enamoured by the gesture he stepped forward placing his hands on her arms and gave her a kiss on the cheek. In a way that a dear acquaintance would be greeted after a long time apart.

Laura was instantly relieved of the awkward hash she had made as an introduction to the evening. She was also pleased to see that Jacob appeared to be reciprocating. "Relax" she thought to herself smiling back at him.

"So, would you prefer coffee? drinks or diner?" he asked, "Perhaps visit a bar before getting something to eat?" he added.

"That sounds wonderful" she replied. He held out his arm for her to take which she did. "Right, this way then" he said leading the way, "Now Miss Appleton, tell me more about your fantastic work".

They rounded the corner onto Cross Street where they continued until arriving at Mr Thomas' chop shop. A quaint traditional English pub dating back as far as 1867 with beautiful Victorian architecture.

Inside they found a cosy red two-person wooden table next to an old fireplace.  Jacob pulled a chair back for Laura to sit, "Why, thank you very much" she said jokingly in an overly posh voice.

"You look lovely," he commented, "the blue of your dress really suits you." Jacob hung his black jacket on the back of his chair and sat down. "What would you like to drink?" he asked.

Laura stumbled ever so slightly on her chair; she was so nervous. Her arms sprung out to steady herself. She was biting her bottom lip and looking up at Jacob grinning.

"Well, that was scary" she said widening her eyes for emphasis of the ordeal.

Jacob had found her quirkiness incredibly endearing.

He said, "Now that you're safe, can I get you something to calm your nerves?"

"Absolutely" she said, "dry white wine please". With that Jacob went to the bar. Laura noted his clothes; he wore smart black shoes with smart black trousers and a navy dress shirt with the sleeves rolled up. Laura noticed they had unknowingly complemented each other. He returned a few moments later with two large glasses of wine – one white and one red. "My hero" she said as he placed down her glass.

Her nerves soon left her. They got on immediately and the conversation didn't pause for a second. Twenty minutes later they left Mr Thomas' and continued along Cross street until taking a left on King Street towards Rosso restaurant.

Jacob held the door for her as they entered the restaurant and walked the short corridor to the concierge. "Mr. Rivers, so nice to have you with us this evening, have you booked?" asked the concierge. Laura shot Jacob a puzzled look as he replied, "Sorry Stephen, no, do you have a table for two?" "We always have room for you sir" Stephen said and motioned for a waitress to guide them to a seat. The waitress was young and slim, with high cheekbones and flawless skin. She had long dark brown hair in a ponytail and matching dark brown eyes. Her top shirt buttons were undone exposing her collarbone. She led them to a table. "I'll be back in a few minutes to take your orders, sir" said the waitress as she handed them the menus, eyeing Jacob slowly before firing Laura a look and turning to attend to another table.

Laura could not help but wrinkle her nose and give the unwitting waitress a scowl. She caught Jacob looking at her with an amused yet puzzled expression. "Something wrong?" he asked glancing over to the waitress then back to Laura. "Could she be more obvious, she was all over you! I'm sat right here!" she said. Jacob decided to play coy. "Nonsense" he said pretending to read the menu "she was simply being attentive ". He grinned as Laura gave him an unamused look.

A few seconds passed as they perused the menus before Laura asked in a mocking accusing tone "Did you bring me here to impress me Mr. Rivers?" Jacob looked up from his menu to meet her eyes and raised his eyebrows. "Impress you?" he repeated bemused. "Yes Mr. Rivers, of course Mr. Rivers, take me home for dessert Mr. Rivers". She said with a wry grin. "That all depends" he said. "On what?" she asked quizzically. He kept eye contact "Is it working?" Moments later, the waitress returned to take their drinks order "For madam?" she asked. "I will have...a dry white wine please" said Laura. "And for you sir?" asked the waitress playing with her hair brazenly flirting. Laura's eyes flitting from the waitress to Jacob "A Tempranillo please" he said, "Very well" said the waitress and she turned and left to get their drinks. "Well, she's in need of some humility" Said Laura. "She certainly is" remarked Jacob returning his attention to the menu. "She also needs to realize; she can't hold a candle to you" he added as a matter of fact. He looked up and caught her eye; she could not help but smile.

"So, tell me more about Laura Appleton" Jacob said, and he took a sip of wine. "Well, where to begin" she said. "Ok, so I was born in Chiswick. I am 34 years

old. I have a younger sister called Lily. I moved here a few months ago to concentrate on my photography career. I like cooking, music, films, books, traveling. I am close to my mum Janet. My dad passed a few years ago..." she paused to take a drink. "I'm sorry to hear that" said Jacob. "Thanks, its fine" she said, "he was killed during an altercation outside a pub."
"That's terrible; did they catch the person responsible?" Asked Jacob. "Well yes and no, they held some bloke called Gregory Malcolm but let him go saying they didn't have sufficient evidence for prosecution." Jacob's heart stopped. "Are you ok?" asked Laura catching his reaction. "Y-yes I'm fine" he said regaining his composure. "I can't believe they let the suspect go" he took a gulp of wine.
She continued "it was hard, mum was angry for so long. I should probably call her actually... I just hope karma catches up with whoever was responsible." Jacob smiled "I'm sure it will, if it hasn't already" he said. "Please excuse me" he said. "Oh of course" said Laura, raising her glass in jest.
With Jacob gone, Laura took in her surroundings with her photographer's eye. The restaurant was very classy. White walls, some with artwork. All the tables were stylishly draped in white tablecloths with matching white chairs. There was a dome in the ceiling which was lit with blue light adding a wonderful ambience to the room. "Yes," Laura thought to herself, "this will do nicely."
In the restroom Jacob dialled his control. Extension please?" "0502" Jacob replied. Rainbow, Grey Wolf" he said. "One moment sir". After two rings Rainbow answered, Jacob could hear a party in the background. "Hello? Grey wolf?" Asked Rainbow. "I need you to refund the last payment to

the beneficiary in full." Jacob said, "you keep your commission I'll pay the outstanding amount." After a brief pause Rainbow finally spoke "you sure? This is quite unprecedented!". "Yes, I am sure, please process as soon as you can and pass on my sincere compliments. Enjoy your party"

With that he rang off and returned to the table. "So, you didn't sneak out the restroom window after all" said Laura with a smile. "Certainly not" he said frowning at the thought.

"So, tell me about you" said Laura raising her eyebrows indicating her intrigue. "Where to begin?" He started "I was born in Kent, to a lovely couple called Vanessa and David. When I was about seven, they were involved in an incident which ultimately cost them their lives." Laura raised a hand to cover her mouth in shock. Jacob shook his hand to indicate it was fine. "From there I went from foster home to foster home. Kept my head down in school and mostly kept to myself. I found comfort and companionship in books and particularly in art." "What happened to your parents?" Asked Laura reaching her hand over the table and placing it on his. "Close to Christmas, someone broke into the house. My parents went to intervene, he had a knife" He could see the concern on her face. "It's in the past now and I've dealt with it. So anyway, I went to college then university and moved up here much for the same reasons as you." At that moment, the house lights dipped adding a more romantic atmosphere and the waitress returned to take their order.

The food was fantastic, the wine and conversation flowed. It had been an incredibly long time since Jacob had felt like this. He felt like a new man. They stepped out the restaurant, cool air filled their lungs. They stood close. "So, what would you say if we were to continue our discussion on modern art back at my place?" Laura asked pointing up the street. "That sounds like a great idea" said Jacob "lead the way".

Twenty minutes later they were at Laura's flat, Jacob sat in the lounge. "I have beer in the fridge or wine if you'd prefer" she shouted from the kitchen. "Wine would be great". He said. A moment later she returned with two glasses. She placed them on the table and sat next to him. It was a small couch. As Laura sat, Jacob could feel her legs against his. She was close. She held her glass of wine in toast and said "To... meeting new people and trying new things". She tilted her head appearing thoughtful. Jacob lent forward and kissed her. His heart felt as though it had swollen in his chest. He raised a hand to cradle her head as she placed a hand on his face. He sat back, feeling vulnerable for the first time in his life. Laura slowly placed her wine glass down on the table and stood. She reached out and took His hand. She Stepped back slightly, and he stood to meet her. She looked at him sheepishly and then led him to the bedroom.

In Chiswick, the phone rang distracting Janet from her book. "Hello?" She said answering the phone. "Hello Mrs Appleton, I'm calling about an account you opened recently with a deposit of eighty thousand?" said the stranger. "Oh, yes?" Said Janet caught off guard. "Well, I was just calling to let you know that the account has been closed and we will be refunding you the full amount". "I don't understand" said Janet starting to panic "closed? Why?" Rainbow continued "Mrs Appleton, your account has been successfully closed in a most satisfactory and fitting way. The operative wishes to pass on his sincere compliments along with a full refund but I can assure you the account has been successfully closed. We wish you the best in your future endeavours." And with that he rang off. Janet sat staring at the phone, both elated and bewildered.

•••

Sunday morning Jacob lay awake, watching Laura as she slept. He couldn't quite believe the twist of fate he had been dealt. He had the privilege of ridding the world of the very person that had caused her such harm. He began to wonder, had he known would he have drawn it out longer? Perhaps made him suffer more? He knew he should not get personal about it. It was done and he should be happy in the knowledge that he was able to provide justice, closure, revenge. She was so peaceful. Beautiful. He knew things were going to be different moving forward, but he sensed a great hope and excitement. "Let's not get ahead of ourselves" he thought. "She may wake to regret this". At that moment she opened her eyes and smiled, happy to see him. She moved herself over toward him. Thigh across his legs, arm around his waist and head on his chest. Jacob put his arms around her and kissed her forehead.

# CHAPTER 3

Martyn Barber had a lucky escape. He had been a prolific scam artist who fled town whenever things got too heated. Recently he had carried out one of his most daring schemes; targeted at the elderly, he had gone from home to home with an elaborate plan as to how he could ensure their financial safety. When met with resistance he would engage in harassment tactics. This would include anything from verbal to physical abuse to visiting victim's property during the night to leave the occupant in fear for their lives. Recently he had made a killing both literally and figuratively. In total his latest round of scams had landed him the tidy sum of nearly seventy-five thousand pounds. Leaving several vulnerable people near penniless. One older Gentleman by the name of John Wardle, a world war 2 veteran, sadly died due to the harassment and shock of what he had undergone. As such Mr. Wardle's eldest son, with the help of a certain member of the law enforcement agency, had submitted a request to the committee. Rainbow was happily processing the application which he earmarked for Grey wolf. The issue was that sadly the bounty for this was rather low as the requestor was unfortunately not very well off following recent events because of Mr. Barber.

Martyn Barber was currently enjoying a life of luxury in Chorlton. Where he enjoyed fine wine, fine dining, nights out and an assortment of debauched activities involving Rohypnol.

Rainbow completed his job sheet and uploaded it to the server and sent Grey wolf the usual notification.

•••

The sound of the vibrating phone caught Jacob's attention. After a slow start to the day, both he and Laura had opted to go to a cafe for breakfast. He saw a message from anonymous which read "debt collectors wanted, apply now". He smirked, although he had never met Rainbow, he enjoyed his cryptic messages that would somehow relate to whatever the new task was.

He had finished his scrambled egg on toast and was now enjoying a black coffee while Laura was halfway through her full English. "So, I meant to ask you, what was all that last night in the restaurant?" She asked. "All what?" He said, "The Mr. Rivers stuff" She said and gave him a look as if to say -explain yourself". "Ok, the jig is up. I supplied their artwork. I met most of them a few times for selection and installation. Your waitress friend not included." "You sold them paintings?" She asked, "and they treat you like lord of the manor?" "No, no" he countered "they commissioned me to create original pieces, that was my work hanging in there" he said. Laura's mouth dropped open amazed. "Shut up!" She exclaimed "Really? You dark horse! Ok now I want to know what other secrets you are hiding. Tell me, who is this mysterious Jacob Rivers before me?" She said narrowing her eyes for emphasis. I'm an art dealer who seduces his clients" he said jokingly before taking another sip of his coffee. "A true rascal!" Laura said pointing accusingly at him "anymore deep dark secrets you'd like to share?" Jacob looked her in the eye a slight smirk on his face "In my spare time I'm also a part time assassin." He said. "You?" She laughed "Now that is hilarious".

Just then Jacob overheard the news report on the cafe Radio; "On Saturday morning police were called to the scene of a Bentley found burned out in the Ardwick area..." Jacob smiled.

•••

Martyn Barber forced his way in through the door. Valerie fell over backwards as he pushed passed. She had answered a knock at the door and unexpectedly welcomed in a demon. "Get out of my house!" She demanded, arthritic finger pointing at him in anger while she sat on the floor. "Money!" He shouted at her, raising a fist "where is your money?"

"How dare you!" She screamed. Still sat on the floor. Valerie had recently enjoyed her 86th birthday. Her family: both daughters with their husbands and her grandchildren had visited her at her home and there had been a great fuss with cake, music, a little brandy and laughter. All a distant memory as the demon with a monkeys' face violated her home.

Her whole head hurt. He had punched her hard and she raised a shaky hand to her cheek. "In the dresser, in the bedroom" she cried. He made his way into the bedroom and began pulling out the drawers from the dresser. A few minutes later he shot passed her as she lay sobbing on the hallway floor.

Before the end of the morning, all two hundred- and thirty-pounds Martyn had stolen was lost to the bookies in Ladbrokes.

That afternoon, back at his house Jacob did his best to catch up on his usual routine. It had been a wonderful night and a lovely morning but now there was a task which needed his attention. He logged on to the server to see the uploaded file.

Job reference: 630
Name: Martyn Barber
Year of birth 1980
Height: 5ft 6"
Contract: Exclusive.
Method: Open
Vehicle: Currently unknown.
Offenses: Assault, robbery and fraud of the elderly. Verified.
Expiration date: Earliest convenience
Location: Domestic. Manchester, Chorlton area.

Remuneration: 30k
Accept -reply 5 / Reject- reply 8.

Jacob looked at the mug shot. Martyn was a short thin white man with a beer gut. His face reminded Jacob of a monkey particularly the way his ears stuck out. He clenched his jaw as he re-read the rap sheet.
"Taking advantage of the bloody elderly!" He thought in disgust.
He texted the number five to the anonymous number then immediately made the call to Rainbow.
"Grey Wolf. I hope you are well this Sunday afternoon. How may I help?"
"Intel" said Jacob, "I'd like to deal with this one swiftly."
Rainbow replied, "you know, I really wasn't sure you would take this one given the bounty."

"The bounty has never been the deciding factor for me Rainbow. In fact, aside from the returned bounty for the last job, every penny of every job I have taken since I started has gone to charity. It goes to one that is related to victims of that perpetrator's offense. That way the irony is that the criminal pays for their crimes not just with their lives, but their death also goes on to help those affected by their transgressions."

"Oh, my boy!" said Rainbow awestruck, "how beautifully poetic". He continued; "Our friend is a creature of habit, bookies, bars and restaurants around the Chorlton area. Word is when he is not preying on the elderly, he enjoys a bit of Theatre. He's attending a production at the Royal Exchange Theatre on Tuesday evening at 7pm."

"Pleasure as always Rainbow" said Jacob and he rang off.

Sitting back, still surprised from Jacobs revelation, Rainbow placed his feet on the corner of his desk, crossing his right foot atop of his left. The heel of his black loafer slipped off his bare right foot as he tapped his foot in the air. Sipping his coffee, he smiled as he admired the latest artwork he had recently purchased.

# CHAPTER 4

Monday was beautiful. Manchester had been blessed
with a near clear blue sky and mild temperature. The
sunlight aided in showing off the stunning array of
architecture the city had on offer and no one had a
better view of the city than Talib Abayoe.
'Tal' as he was known, lived in an ultramodern
penthouse on the forty-sixth floor of Beetham Tower.
Tal's penthouse featured neon lighting throughout, an
enclosed balcony space complete with AstroTurf
floor, stylish interior and the architect himself as his
upstairs neighbour.

Talib was making his final preparations for the day.
He was dressed in a light grey turtleneck, dark skinny
fit cropped trousers, lilac suit jacket and black loafers
without socks. Aside from his pencil moustache he
was clean shaven and kept his hair short and neat with
a high fade. He loved fashion, art, dancing and had a
passion for all things unique.
He checked himself in the mirror and, happy with his
flawless appearance, he applied a liberal helping of
Dolce and Gabanna perfume. "Spray, delay and walk
away" he said to himself as he glided through the
descending mist. On his way out the door he noticed
one of his favourite paintings was crooked. "This will
not do!" He said adjusting the surrealist oil painting
of a rainbow landscape by J. Rivers. "There, much
better". With that he left the apartment and
summoned a lift.

Jacob had made an early start. He had planned to
meet Laura for lunch and wanted to complete the

frames before she arrived. They were dry and he was about to begin the final stages of framing, but the shop had been unusually busy that morning. He had sold two paintings, one of which was his own, making a tidy profit of around eight thousand pounds before midday.

One by one he lay each frame face down on the workbench with a plush towel beneath them to protect them from scratches. He began pre-drilling the holes for the metal clips to be attached in-order to hold the back board in place and the D-rings to hold the hanging wire. He placed the large, printed photographs into the frame, inserted the back board then fastened the clips and added the D-rings. Once secured he threaded the picture wire giving each of the six pictures a meticulous framer wrap. He finished each one with a tension pull to relieve any slack on the wire.

He could not wait to show Laura. He positioned them on the wall of the framing studio as he normally would for a client to observe his handy work. Just then he heard the intercom buzz and a familiar voice say "Sweetie? Where are you my boy, I'm in need of something fresh!" Jacob smiled, he always enjoyed his visits from Talib, and he knew just what to show him.

Moments later Jacob was leading Laura across the shop towards the framing area where she recognised the stylish tall black gentleman from her last visit, although this time without the distinctive fedora. "Ah, this must be the fabulous Miss Laura Appleton I've heard so much about," he exclaimed with a smile and extended an arm to welcome her into the room.

"Laura, this is Mr. Talib Abayoe" Jacob said, "Tal, please may I introduce the fabulously talented and beautiful, Miss Laura Appleton". Tal took Laura's hand saying, "So you're the reason my boy Jacob here has such a glow about him." Jacob rolled his eyes as Laura blushed and shrugged her shoulders. Tal and I were just admiring some wonderful work here" said Jacob gesturing to the hanging work. Looking back at Laura both Tal and Jacob saw the look on her face change as she realized it was her work. "Oh my God!" She said beaming, "that's my work! It looks amazing!"

"I hate to spoil the surprise Jacob, but I think she likes it" said Tal jokingly adding "Now Laura, photographer extraordinaire, tell me when and where I can claim one, if not all of these pieces!".

"Well, I'm being included in a Maxus exhibition next week" she said. "I'll send you the details, Tal" Jacob said with a nod. The three of them turning back to view the work.

# CHAPTER 5

It had been a slow start for Martyn. He had been out late last night drinking cocktails in the popular night spot called Revolution de Cuba. It had been busy for a Monday evening and he was having good night. That was until his unwitting victim was carried out to a taxi by one of her friends. He had been working on her for some time, had her cock blocking friend kept her nose out, he would have had his merry way with her once the Rohypnol had worked its magic. Alas that was not to be, so instead he consoled himself with more alcohol.

His day ahead was simple. As it was signing on day, he would go to the dole office first to make sure he received his benefits. He would then call in to his local to spend the afternoon sipping lager and playing on the fruit machine. Later he would grab some fish and chips before heading into Manchester to see "Scenes from the Luddite rebellion".

Without a care in the world, he went about his day.

•••

Jacob had been busy wrapping Laura's work in preparation for the Maxus exhibition and storing them in the basement for safe keeping. On Monday he would close the shop early to deliver the selection to the venue where he'd assist in their display and also work with the evaluator to determine an approximate value of each piece. With Laura's blessing he would use his art dealers' skills to do his best to encourage a few sales, win over any critics and help persuade coverage from the attending reviewers. After all,

Laura would have enough on her plate doing meet and greets, discussing her concepts, perhaps some interviews if things went well.

Through the day he mulled over his latest assignment. Now more than ever he was considering how much longer he wished to continue being involved in these affairs – meeting Laura had changed this. Over the years, however his efforts had brought closure to those in need and saved others from falling victim. "Maybe a couple more" he thought. While in the basement again he went to the locked chest and retrieved a new pair of leather gloves, his gun belt, gun, ankle knife and a length of cord.

•••

Laura has been on the phone to her mother for nearly an hour filling her in on all her news. She had noticed a change in her mother. A good change, for the longest time since her dad had died her mother sounded happy, jubilant and full of life again. "Mum, I know you're pleased about coming to my first exhibit but what's happened? You are freaking me out a bit. Mum, please tell me honestly... are you on drugs?" She asked in mocked seriousness. Janet laughed "No Laura! Don't be silly! I have just come into a bit of luck that is all. I got something that I'd been seeking for a long time". she said. "What was that?" Asked Laura. "Closure" Janet replied smiling to herself. "Now tell me about this new boyfriend of yours..."

He sat in the back row of the theatre. On the stage the actors were nearing the climax of their impassioned performance. The performance area itself was a curious design Jacob appreciated. It was circular, almost like an amphitheatre with the stage in the centre on the floor. From the outside, the structure resembled Apollo 11 which sat beneath one of the remaining domes of the Exchange building ceiling. The dome, the space, the floor to ceiling pillars all have an air of opulence and a true feast for the eyes and played a part in the spectacle.

The actors bowed. The crowd cheered. A tale of Northern grit.

As the patrons made their way out, Jacob kept his eye on his target from a distance. Making his way down the yellow staircase, Martyn went straight to the Rivals bar in the foyer where he ordered a double vodka and coke. Jacob sat in the outside courtyard area with lights strung between streetlamps. There are a few tables with checked tablecloths giving it a romantic air of a European square. He took a seat within eyesight of his mark and ordered a black coffee.

Martyn sat head bowed scrolling through his phone. After a while he sipped his drink then made a call. Jacob listened carefully as Martyn babbled utter nonsense to whoever was on the line. Martyn shifted in his seat surveying the foyer as he told of his latest escapades by where he blew over two hundred pounds on horses.

An hour and three more double vodkas later, Martyn was on his way home. Jacob followed him to St Peter's square where he boarded the tram. Jacob refrained from joining the platform until the tram was on its way into the station to remain out of site for as long as he could. On board, he sat at the opposite end of the carriage as he suspected the target would exit at the next stop in approximately twenty-four minutes at Chorlton. Once again Martyn sat scrolling through his phone thumbing through his Tinder account to see if there was anyone worth date raping.

Eventually the tram pulled in and Martyn alighted with, Jacob following at a safe distance. Surveillance and counter surveillance came naturally to him. Martyn made his way up Buckingham Road, and on to Bryan Road where he lived. Jacob watched him enter his home and then waited twenty minutes for Martyn to get comfortable before he made his move.

•••

"Who the fuck is that!" Martyn whined as he stood to answer the door. He wiped the cocaine from his nostrils and paused the porn on the TV. He quickly tucked himself away and refastened his trousers. Opening the door, he was confused by the stranger who stood at his door. "Yeah, what?" He said his face contorted in frustration. "Welcome to redemption" Jacob said smiling. "What the f-...." before he could finish, his legs went from beneath him. He thought he may throw up and he did not feel as though he could breathe. Jacob had delivered a colossal kick to his testicles rendering him temporarily incapacitated. He entered the property closing the front door behind him.
Martyn knelt on the floor, his hands cupping his groin "W-w-who are you...w-what do you want?". Jacob noted the panicked breaths. "You've been a bit of a

nuisance to a lot of elderly people, they want their pound of flesh".

He did not even see it coming, quick as lighting Jacob connected a haymaker to Martyn's left temple. The sound as it connected was truly satisfying. A nice hard thwack. Jacob had got the measure of his opponent. He was a strongman when it came to bullying the infirm but when it came down to it; Martyn Barber was a weak, pathetic, snivelling piece of shit.

Without wasting time Jacob seized the opportunity, moving behind Martyn and pulling the cord out from his jacket pocket. With a length between his hands, he used it as a garrotte slipping it around Martyn's neck. Jacob crossed the ends of the cord and wrapped it around his neck a second time to ensure Martyn's air waves were sufficiently restricted. Martyn's hands clawed helplessly at his neck. His eyes wide and his mouth open, in a futile struggle for air.

Holding the cord in one fist, Jacob lifted Martyn from the floor and looked him in the eye. "You deserve much worse than this. For the lives you ruined. For the pain you caused. Do you understand?" Jacob said.

Martyn, still grasping at his noose shook his head in denial. Jacob dropped him to the ground with a thud. The slight slack of the cord allowing him to steal a few breaths. Jacob landed a perfect blow with the top of his foot to the bridge of Martyn's nose. A blinding white light stealing his vision, his eyes filled with tears. Jacob regained his grip on the cord and dragged his prey up the stairs, thrashing out his legs but unable to scream. When he reached the top, he rounded the bannister lifting the cord stair side and pulling it over the rail. Martyn performed a remarkable airborne samba as Jacob tied the cord to the bannister. Martyn was heavy and Jacob's muscles burned but he was spurred on by the thoughts of those robbed of their life's savings by this parasite. This was for them.

He stood and watched the last moments of Martyn Barber's attempt to cling life.

His face red and swollen. His eyes bulging and bloodshot. His expression was fascinating. It reminded Jacob of "The Scream of Nature" by Edvard Munch.

Martyn hung lifeless from the bannister.

Unperturbed, Jacob made his way downstairs, opened the front door and checked the scene was clear before slipping away.

On his way home he called his control to inform him of the news; "Sorry for the late call Rainbow. Please inform the beneficiary the job is completed. All loose ends are now tied" he said reciprocating Rainbows use of bad puns.

"Oh, I like the sound of that. I will process the payment first thing tomorrow. Good work Grey wolf" replied Rainbow. And with that the call ended. Jacob pulled up his jacket collar as the rain began to fall. "If there is one thing you can bet on, it's the bloody rain" he thought as he made his way home.

# CHAPTER 6

Terry Fletcher sat alone in Charlie's office. He nervously took another cigarette from its box and placed it to his lips. He spun the lighter between his thumb and middle finger, staring into space. The sound of Charlie's voice as he approached brought him back to the room. From the corner of his eye, he saw the door open and Charlie enter talking on his phone. Sitting at his high back leather chair behind his mahogany desk, he nodded at Terry in acknowledgment. "We're talking around fifty-five million" Charlie said in a north-eastern accent. Grinning at the thought of such profit. Terry noticed Charlie's yellow stained teeth and fillings from years of smoking and bad diet. Terry reached a shaky hand to his mouth and removed the cigarette putting it back in the box.

Terry Fletcher had been a good man.

He had spent years serving his country in Her majesty's Northumbrian police force. Attaining the rank of Detective Chief inspector before his dishonourable discharge ten years ago. He had been proud of his promotion and senior rank, but he had spent too much time with the enemy. Eventually he went native and began supplying tip offs and information in return for payments. Most commonly for an up-and-coming gangster by the name of Charlie Hobbs. It would be fair to say that back in the day, Terry was afraid of Charlie, even though he had the protection of the force. Now he no longer had that protection and given Charlie's rise, influence and reach, it would be fair to say he was terrified of him.

He was ashamed of the man he had become. So were his family. His wife left him shortly after his discharge, his daughter was appalled by him. He hadn't seen either of them for several years, which hurt him terribly. It hurt mostly because Terry's time was running out. He had been diagnosed with Amyotrophic lateral sclerosis - a progressive disease that affects nerve cells in the brain and spinal cord. Symptoms usually begin with muscle twitching, limb weakness and slurred speech until eventually it renders the affected person unable to move, eat or breathe. As there is still no cure, Terry hoped to make amends before his time ran out.

Putting down his mobile phone, Charlie looked Terry up and down. "You look like shit Terry." He said, "like you aged fifty years over night."
Terry stared at the floor, like a schoolboy being criticized by a head teacher.
"Howay man! Spit it out!" He said, tapping a Regal cigarette three times on the box before lighting it.
Terry raised his eyes taking in the view that was Charlie Hobbs. Six foot three inches, about eighteen stone, broad shoulders. His arms were enormous. He was a beast of a man. Terry would often joke that he supplied Charlie with steroid filled Greggs pasties for lunch. His light ginger hair was styled in a flat top crew cut making his face have a square appearance. Acne scars marked his face along with a misshapen nose that looked like that of a bare-knuckle boxer.
"It's about Gregory; he's gone off the grid." Said Terry.
"Off the grid? Gregory?" Repeated Charlie.
"He made the deal for the ketamine, then at the weekend his car was found burned out and he went

missing." Terry continued "the Ketamine was in the car when it was torched, it's gone, a whole kilo, thirty thousand pounds. Not to mention the rest of the stash he had on him."

Terry sat still. Hands clasped together waiting. He knew what was about to happen. Charlie would start talking slowly and calmly, and then he would erupt. He kept his head bowed avoiding eye contact, like animals in the wild do to show passiveness, to avoid accidentally challenging the pack alpha. In fact, Charlie was not too far removed from a silverback gorilla.

Charlie cocked his head to the right and flicked the ash from his cigarette into the tray on his desk. "So, you're telling me..." he began quietly "someone robbed Greg's car..." wait for it. "Torched it", wait for it. "Meanwhile that fat bastards done a runner." any minute now... "AND I'M DOWN OVER THIRTY FUCKING GRAND?" He spat.

"We don't know who it was but we're certain it wasn't the new contacts" Terry said meekly.

"Certain? Certain I'll show you fucking certain!" He continued to shout. "Go get me some answers before I start leathering the lot of you!"

It was predictable Charlie. Uncontrollable rage which led to physical threats on everyone within a five-mile radius. The issue was that he always followed through.

Terry was tired, he was so tired. He left Charlie's office and continued out of the building. He got in his car and drove for roughly half an hour until he found a secluded place to pull in and park.

He phoned an old acquaintance.

"Detective inspector Davis." The voice said.

"John, its Terry, mate. Can you still put me in touch with that Committee that helps people, it's time?"
"How long d'ya have?" Asked the inspector.
"Weeks, if I'm lucky" said Terry "not long at all".

# CHAPTER 7

Laura entered the hair salon greeting the staff. "Laura Appleton, I have a 12:30 appointment, with Liz" she said peering over the narrow counter at the appointment book. "Ah yes, Liz will be 2 minutes, just take a seat. Tea, Coffee?" Asked the apprentice. "No, I'm fine" said Laura as she sat down in the waiting area.

She picked up a copy of Hello magazine and leafed through for a few minutes, pulling faces from time to time as she caught salacious headlines and vilifications of various reality nobodies. "What is this crap?" She said to herself dropping the magazine back onto the table as though it had the potential to dirty her hands.

"Laura?" A young lady asked. "I'm ready for you now." She said. Laura smiled politely and followed her to the empty chair. "So, what are you looking to do today?" she asked while looking critically at Laura's hair, moving it about for no apparent reason. "Perhaps maybe some highlights and I was thinking about a fringe, maybe?" Laura said wondering why she was using her right hand in an American style salute to emphasize what she meant.

"Yeah, we can do that" the young lady said as she continued to pull at Laura's hair.

•••

Rainbow had recently returned to his apartment and was enjoying the view from his balcony. He had spent the day shopping and eating lunch with friends, two of his favourite things to do. He had bought some clothes and a Brietling watch. He had a thing for expensive watches. This new piece being the eighth in his collection brought their collective worth to around thirty thousand pounds.

He was extravagant and he knew it, but he did not compromise when it came to luxury. He appreciated the finer things in life and deserved them. From a homeless twelve-year-old Sudanese refugee to a highly educated professional, he had led a turbulent life. Even in the assumed safety of England he faced adversity for being a black homosexual refugee. He loved ballet, visual art, architecture and music by the band Slipknot. Tal "Rainbow" Abayoe was certainly the definition of a tenacious, flamboyant and unique individual.

Relaxing after a busy afternoon, he sat reading 'Things Fall Apart' by Chinua Achebe, sipping pineapple juice with ice and loving life.

•••

Jacob had been at the shooting range for a few hours. There were surprising number of shooting clubs around the Northwest area, which made it easier for Jacob to keep up his skills – they were necessary. He had started with long distance rifle practice using a Weatherby MK V hunting rifle. The Weatherby had a range of around a thousand meters and a five-round capacity, a fearsome bit of equipment. Eventually he moved on to further close-range target practice with the Glock 17 pistol. Later he might paint. He wasn't seeing Laura until the exhibition as she had her mother visiting so he was thinking about how best to occupy his time. He had never had an issue before but lately, he found himself a little lost. "Get a grip of yourself; you're acting like a lovesick schoolboy!" He reprimanded himself only to grin seconds later in acknowledging that is exactly how he felt. Perhaps much later he might read with a glass or two of wine, maybe flick through an art magazine. He may even go to a concert; he was aware Adam Hurt was playing. Perhaps Tal was free? The day was his. He raised his pistol and took aim and gently squeezed the trigger. Within seconds he emptied the magazine of all 17 rounds.

•••

Terry had had another rough night. His body was failing him, and he knew he would soon be in a hospice. Death's waiting room he used to call it. He looked at himself in the mirror. His hair was near white. His face had a line for every lie he had told his wife and child, and he stooped when he walked. He looked older than he was by a decade.  He reminisced about his younger days. He was a fine specimen, lean and athletic. A keen footballer: he nearly played professionally but an injury swiftly ended that dream. How it could have been he thought. He looked up from the sink back to his reflection. His eyes misted with tears. Of all the things he had done, regret would be the biggest weight on his heart. Regret for not being a stronger man. Regret for not treating his wife and daughter better. Regret for squandering his opportunities. With both hands he scooped up warm water from the sink and splashed his face. He applied shaving cream and picked up his razor with a shaky hand, eyes welling up.  Condensation cast a vignette on the mirror. A drop of blood in the water below.

# CHAPTER 8

Jacob managed to get two tickets to see Adam Hurst at The Bridgewater hall. He was one of his favourite musicians. Tal, who had been surprised by the invitation, was also looking forward to a night of cultural indulgence. They had agreed to meet in the Anthologist bar in St Peter's Square, a modern bar with a range of poison for all types. Jacob was early and expected that Tal, despite living relatively near, would still be fashionably late. He decided to use the time to phone Laura who picked up almost straight away. "Hi" he said, "that was quick!"

"I was just texting you; we must have a stronger psychic connection than we realized" she joked adding "so what are your plans tonight? I've got a friend popping over for a few drinks maybe a film."

"Believe it or not" he said, "I'm meeting Tal, we're going to see a concert."

"Ooh boy's night out!" She joked "you'd better behave; I can see Tal getting you into all sorts of trouble."

"I'll be good" he said, "oh he's here, I'd better go. Have a fun night."

"You too! Bye." She rang off.

Standing in the doorway as if he were about to begin his turn on the catwalk, Tal scanned the room. He caught sight of Jacob grinning at him. "Jacob my boy!" He bellowed, hands in the air as though he had been searching for hours. He began his strut towards their table. He was a character thought Jacob. And rather wonderful company at that.

Pauli, however, was having a bad night. He didn't know where he was nor did he know how he got there. His memory of the past couple of days had been scrambled. He was sat in a dark empty room tied to a chair with a single light bulb hanging above his head. His forearms tie wrapped to the chair arms. His ankles shackled to the chair legs. His head hurt. His jaw ached. His ribs were cracked. His clothes were stained in his own blood and he had soiled himself, but he tried to pretend he didn't care. Pauli always liked to play the hard man. Ever since he was twelve, he had walked with his arms out like he was carrying a carpet under each arm. Swearing; spitting, smoking, taking drugs and carrying out antisocial triumphs. Some of his best work included: Shoplifting, smashing bus stops to pieces, beating up unwitting people (but only when he was with his gang), bootlegging pornography and, of course, his latest work with Gregory.

At this moment, however, he didn't feel much like a hard man at all. In fact, he was scared out of his wits. The door opened and a figure entered. It was hard to see. His eyes went wide with dread as he began to see the outline in darkness. He began hyperventilating as the figure slowly stepped forward into full view.

"Alreet Pauli?" Asked Charlie quietly looking down at him. Pauli could do nothing but take in the colossus before him. He began to whimper.

"Shhh, just tell me where Gregory is. Who torched the car?" he said getting louder. "Where are my fucking drugs?" Said Charlie.

"I don't know! I swear I don't know anything!" Said Pauli.

"Where the fuck is Greg!" Charlie suddenly shouted, cracking his knuckles.

Pauli shook his head unable to speak in fear of what was to come. He balled his hands into fists and experienced another wave of warm humiliation as he pissed his pants again.

•••

The atmosphere created between the music and the lights was just spectacular.

Jacob was transfixed by the performance as it built to its climax. He, along with Tal and the rest of the audience, stood in applause of the magnificent production they had witnessed. Tal leant to whisper in Jacobs's ear, "Oh my boy that was fantastic, simply fantastic!" Eventually the applause faded, the house lights came on and people made their way out of the venue. Outside Tal and Jacob made their way back towards St Peter's square for a night cap. "Brooding cello and haunting piano, no wonder you're such a ray of sunshine" Tal said mockingly. "I'm sunny enough I'll have you know" Jacob replied with a smirk. "Ah yes, the delectable Laura Appleton, she looks good on you my boy but we both know you're punching above your weight." Tal continued his banter.

Up ahead five men approached. They were rowdy chanting what Jacob assumed was something to do with football. "I'm telling you" Tal continued "you want to keep hold of that one, she is..."

At that point two of the five men barged into Tal and Jacob.

"You got a problem?" Asked the man who made contact. "Perhaps you are unaware, but you happened to walk into me and my friend here" replied Tal.

Jacob remained focused, hopefully it would lead to

nothing, but he was prepared for an altercation should it come to it.

"You what? You fucking bla..." before the leader could finish his racist slur, Tal had gone low in a technique Jacob had not seen before. He seized the leader by the belt with his left hand with an underarm grip; with his right he lifted the opposite leg bringing the now hapless antagonist off his feet. Tal continued to show impressive strength lifting him higher until he was a meter and a half off the ground. Suddenly Tal slammed him down on his back. The sound of the collision leaving his four friends in collective shock. Winded and pride severely wounded the hapless attacker lay in agony. Hopefully, a lesson learned. Tal stood and straightened his clothes. He made eye contact with the remaining men who stood motionless. Tal took one last look at the assailant before motioning to Jacob that they should take their leave. As they walked away the four louts helped their associate to his feet all the while berating him for his behaviour.

"Interesting take down" Jacob remarked "what was that technique you used?"

"Oh" Tal said "Nuba, Sudanese wrestling."

"Certainly effective. Drink?" Said Jacob.

"Oh, my boy yes! The night has just begun!" Tal said as he beamed a beautiful huge smile.

•••

It was close to midnight. Pauli had a broken jaw and fractured left eye socket. His fingernails had been removed by pliers. He hung on death's even horizon. Charlie breathed heavily, arms turned out, his head raised, and his eyes closed as though he was absorbing the life force seeping from Pauli's destroyed body. Confident now that Pauli truly had no idea what had come to pass, Charlie lowered his head and looked at the bloody mess that remained tied to the chair. In a soft voice he said "Alreet Pauli lad, don't worry. I believe you". Pauli lay slumped. He tried to speak but could only produce a mumble as blood dribbled from his mouth to his chest. Obviously, there was no way he could put Pauli back in circulation after this. If he were to recover, he would certainly be of little to no use to anyone. Charlie picked up a lead pipe from the floor giving it a shake to confirm its solid composition. "Can't have you going to hospital like this marrow, police would be all over you. Ta-Ra you bastard." Said Charlie raising the pipe into the air. Like a metal worker hammering glowing metal straight. From the furnace, Charlie rhythmically pummelled Pauli's head in.

# CHAPTER 9

The next morning, Jacob was carrying out maintenance of his house and garden. He would speak to Laura later and see how she was feeling about the exhibit the following day. He was also keen to hear about her mother. If she was happy. If in some way his actions had provided her with the closure, she needed to be able move on with her life in whatever way she could. His garden now looking professionally landscaped, Jacob returned the garden tools to the shed and went inside.

He placed an old towel on the dining table along with a few rags and a bottle of gun oil. He placed down his Glock and Weatherby MK V rifle from his home collection. Before he began, he walked over to his record player; selected a record, removed it from its sleeve. He gently placed it down on the turntable. With a hook of his index finger, he lifted the stylus and placed it in one of the grooves near the edge of the disc. There was a satisfying crackle before music filled the air. He sat and enjoyed the meditation before him.

•••

Talib had spent the morning at 'Bin the gym' on Deansgate. After a challenging high intensity interval training circuit, he was spent but satisfied. He picked up his towel from the floor and placed it over his head taking deep breaths. The instructor was shouting out praise to the class as the smell of hot sticky bodies hung heavy in the air, "Good work Tal see you next week." Tal made for the door raising a hand to say 'thanks and yes be seeing you' as he continued to catch his breath.

Outside, the cool air instantly refreshed him. He headed for home to shower, dress in something comfortable and enjoy a leisurely afternoon.

As he stood awaiting the lift within his building, he was aware of another man standing near him. The doors opened and he looked as to politely indicate he was giving way to the fellow passenger. The stranger smiled politely and entered, Tal following. The pair stood at opposite corners of the lift as the doors slowly closed.

"Do you live in the building?" Asked the stranger.

"Yes, I do, you?" Replied Tal.

"Yes, I recently moved in, I'm on thirty-nine. Great view. I'm Andrew by the way, Andrew Wynn." he said introducing himself and extending a hand.

Tal taking his hand said "Tal Abayoe, very pleased to meet you."

•••

At two-thirty-five in the afternoon an Avanti train pulled into Manchester Piccadilly train station. Laura waited outside the barriers with an eager smile on the face. She had not seen her mother in quite some time. She pulled a fist to her chest and jumped waving her right hand in the air in giddy excitement as Janet came into view. Once out of the throng of commuters Laura and Janet greeted each other with a long hug.

"Hi, how was your journey?" asked Laura.

"Fine said Janet, the train was filthy but nothing unusual."

Janet was just over five foot, with an asymmetric brunette bob hair style. Although diminutive, Janet was by no means a wall flower and was quick of mind and of whit and she had a tongue as sharp as any Japanese sword ever made. She was not one to be trifled with.

"Right let's go, are you hungry?" Asked Laura.

"Famished where do you suggest?" replied Janet.

Laura led the way out of the bustling station, but the pair chatted and caught up the whole way.

•••

Rebecca Trafford sat in her conservatory. The doors were open to let the air in. Her cat lay on a nearby chair in a neat circular slumber.

It had been a difficult hour, listening to the life and crimes of a despicable individual. Rebecca wasn't squeamish in the slightest - as a senior agent in the National Crime Agency, there was little left that she had not either seen or heard. – But this case was different. It was sensitive due to the condition of the informant, clearly dying and attempting to deliver a near deathbed confession in the hope of last-minute absolution. If true, the outlook was terrible. Years of work, her work of shutting down organized crime and stopping the country from being overrun with drugs would lie in ruins. She had some difficult decisions to make. She also knew she would need approval from a higher source if she were to deal with this swiftly.

She thanked Terry Fletcher for his bravery in coming forward and for his time, particularly for the evidence to follow.

As she ended the call, she stared out into the garden to gather her thoughts. The project she had developed years ago called "The committee" had proven its effectiveness but now it needed government immunity if she were to succeed in bringing an end to

Charlie Hobbs. For the sake of Great Britain, it was time for the Committee to be approved and implemented by Her Majesty's Secret Service.

# CHAPTER 10

Laura was nervous. Today was the day. She had phoned Jacob a few times now. Firstly, to make sure he was awake. Secondly, to see if she needed to do anything, and once again to see how things were going. Jacob had received similar calls in the past from other exhibiting artists. He knew it was a nerve-racking experience, even more so when it was a collective of artists - each hoping to outshine the competition. Each artist's work would be judged not only on its own merit but also against the other work on display.

Jacob had arrived early. He managed to sweet talk the event coordinator into letting him install Laura's work in the best possible spot. Work would be placed around the perimeter of the room but, in the centre, there was a large U-shaped Partition, and he took the flat wall directly opposite the entrance. The lighting was perfect and Laura's work, all six photographs would be the first thing everyone saw when they entered. Therefore, not only were they guaranteed to be seen they would also set the tone that the other work would then be judged by.

The venue was stunning. A grade 2 listed building in the Edwardian baroque style. First opened in 1903, the Midland was a perfect venue. The exhibit was to be held in the opulent Darby suite. Often used for such events as well as weddings, it had an ethereal feel to it. A large rectangular room bathed in white and soft cream with a chandelier in the centre of the ceiling. It comfortably held one hundred and fifty people normally giving visitors ample room to mingle and take in the splendour of the event.

As he was finishing setting up Laura's display and adding name plates beneath each work showing the artist's name and the title of the piece, his evaluator arrived. "Tom, great to see you!" Jacob said with a firm handshake. "You too Jacob. So, this is the work you have been so emphatic about." Tom said as he stepped back to take in each image. "You know Jacob; you have a wonderful eye for this kind of thing. Right then, let us get started".

•••

"It has been authorized, time to do the paperwork and make it official. I will be contacting the preferred employees for the strike team in due course. In the meantime, we need Intelligence on where and when to strike. This is not a rehearsal; we need this done right." Rebecca said firmly.

The government agent replied "Understood" and with that the call ended. It had been a remarkable day. The Committee was now an official branch of her Majesty's Secret Service. Rebecca's project was a success and had realised its full potential.

Armed with the highest backing, unlimited finance, intelligence and access to weaponry. The Committee was a domestic agency to be reckoned with. There was only one further task. To select the finest personnel currently on the books and make them official agents.

Of all twelve current members, she would only need six in total. In her portfolio she had a selection of preferred candidates but with other work going on in the country she would concentrate on selecting a two-man strike team to deal with Charlie Hobbs. She liked the look of a long-standing assassin with a faultless record by the name of Jacob 'Grey wolf' Rivers and a new applicant from the control board with impressive credentials; Talib 'Rainbow' Abayoe. Rainbow had a lot of potential and, with Grey Wolf's guidance; the pair would be a formidable duo. Rebecca had received a compelling letter from Tal wishing to progress from control to active duty. With slim choice for recruitment and some less than favourable recruits Rebecca saw the benefit in new field agents being paired with experienced operatives to help show them the ropes. After all this wasn't a run of the mill organisation and the job was not something you could take a course on. Indeed, this could work nicely.

•••

The taxi pulled up right outside the main entrance to the Midland. Laura paid the fare and stepped out holding the door for Janet. Mother and daughter walked up the stairs with suitcases in tow as the doormen nodded in polite greeting ushering them in.

They handed their luggage over to the concierge for safe keeping and followed the signs to the Derby suite. As the doors swung open, Laura was greeted by the sight of her work standing pride of place. She beamed with happiness. By the works, talking to one of the hotel staff was Jacob. He was wearing a charcoal three-piece suit with a white shirt and black wool knit tie. "Jacob!" shouted Laura as the staff member went about her business. Jacob turned to see Laura looking captivating. She was wearing a black Christopher Kane style dress with red matt heeled shoes. Her hair was a lighter shade and she now had a fringe – it suited her. "Laura, you look incredible!" he said. He gave her a hug and a kiss before she turned and said "Jacob, this is my mum, Janet". "Very pleased to meet you" he said. "You too Jacob! I've heard so much about you" said Janet. Together they looked at the display. "I've asked someone to get maintenance here as soon as possible, there is a light on its way out which keeps blinking" Jacob said pointing to a spotlight. "This is wonderful Jacob, thank you so much" Laura said. "Not at all" he replied smiling at her pleased she was happy.

"Can I get either of you a drink to calm the nerves?" he asked.

Laura looked to her mother and said "Champagne?" "It would be rude not to" Janet Said with a smile.

An hour later the venue was packed. People from all walks of life were sipping champagne whilst discussing the various delights on display. The artists providing answers to viewer's questions on every subject from techniques to equipment and inspiration. While Laura was discussing lighting with some aspiring photographers, Jacob was on a mission. He was identifying and engaging the writers from the magazines covering the event and steering them Laura's way. He spoke with writers from; Aesthetica, Pylot, Art Review and Accent to name a few. His charm was working as, one by one; they made their way over to see the works of Miss Appleton. Once Jacob had worked his magic on the critics it was time to target the buyers.

They say there is always one in every crowd and, indeed, he had made his way over to Laura. A young pompous man dressed in his finest Beatnik fashions, determined to inform Laura that her angles and shadows were not as they should be. He seemed to be enjoying the sound of his own voice and was speaking rather loudly while Laura bit her lip and kept her composure.

"This one particularly, low-key photography simply hides the subject, I mean what is..." before he could finish a deep confident voice cut him off, "This beautiful work is down to subjective interpretation my boy, using dark tones, high contrast and minimal lighting. Plus, this one has already been sold Mr.?"

"Thomas Chadwick" the Beatnik replied. "Mr. Chadwick if you please, where can I find your work in this wonderful exhibition?" It was Tal and he motioned to the room with his right hand while his left held a champagne flute. "W-well, I'm not displaying any work here, I don't do commercial events..." said Thomas. "Is that so?" Asked Tal. Winking at Laura and pulling out his phone he continued "Please, what is your website? I'm curious to see what the world is missing?"

Thomas knew when to quit. "Please excuse me" he said retreating to another area only to begin chiding another artist.

Laura gave Tal a hug. "Ooh I. was so close to telling him where to go!" She said. Just then Janet returned from her tour of the room. "Mum, this is Tal" said Laura making introductions. "Wonderful to meet you" Janet said. "The pleasure is mine Mrs. Appleton, your daughter has produced some lovely work, this one in particular" he said pointing to an image of a nude female sitting with arms raised and entwined, her face in shadow as her hair cascaded down. "This, I am pleased to say will sit on my wall as I am the proud owner of an original Appleton." He smiled as he looked at the piece genuinely pleased.

"Laura dear, I'm afraid I'm going to have to make tracks, my taxi to the station is due any minute. Well done though I'm so proud of you!" Said Janet as mother and daughter hugged and kissed goodbye.
"Thank you so much for coming" said Laura.
"Of course! Good luck with the rest of the night, say goodbye to Jacob for me and it was nice to meet you Tal." Janet said as the hugged Laura again and rushed off left to collect her luggage and catch her taxi to the station. "She seems lovely, can I adopt her?" Tal said.

As Janet hurried across the hotel reception, she caught site of Jacob making his way toward her smiling warmly, "taking you leave?" He asked. "Yes, off to catch the train, lovely meeting you" she said. "You too! Have a safe and pleasant journey" Jacob said and watched as she made her way outside. He had never knowingly met a beneficiary before. She really did seem happy. He took pride in being able to help.

By the end of the night, five of the six of Laura's Works had been sold with the remaining one to be placed in Jacobs shop. Laura was dizzy with the buzz of the night. The event staff would store the work until payments had been made and each piece would be shipped to their respective residences.

As Laura and Jacob were talking, they were joined by Joan Willis. Jacob greeted Joan with a kiss on each cheek. They had been long time acquaintances. "Joan, good to see you again" said Jacob.

"Jacob, you're looking well, Laura congratulations I believe you've had a great night" Joan said, "Yes it's been quite a night, thanks again for choosing my work." Said Laura. "Not at all Laura, in fact I want to discuss further events if you're interested? I'll call you later in the week to discuss" Turning to Jacob she said "I'll be in touch with you soon as well, great to see you both. Must dash" Joan said before swiftly making the rounds.

"Wow" said Laura, "what an incredible night!" She threw her arms around Jacob and squeezed him. After a few moments enjoying the comfort of each other and the stillness, Jacob said, "shall we?"

"Yes, we shall" said Laura. With that they collected Laura's luggage from reception and made their way to his car. "My god Jacob" Laura said seeing his car for the first time. A huge smile on her face. "What do you do in this thing fight wars while driving up mountains?" She laughed. "Sometimes, you have to be prepared for World War 3, In the meantime I commute to work" he joked. They settled into the cabin and fastened their seatbelts. "Homeward" he said turning the key in the ignition, looking at Laura as she smiled back at him.

Late that night they arrived at Jacob's house. Laura was instantly impressed with the property. She loved the open plan living space, especially the large windows. The interior was minimalist and sophisticated. Jacob got them both a glass of wine and they sat in the lounge. They were both tired but elated with how the night had gone.

Here. Now. Together. There was peace and calm. Everything as it should be. She was close, his arm around her. He could smell her perfume as studied her face as she spoke. As if trying to commit every feature to memory. He wanted to make up for the time he had not known her. He was falling for her and falling hard. He began playing with her hair that fell by her shoulder. He loved listening to her too; she was Witty, intelligent and eloquent.

Laura herself was lost in a train of thought. She had found something with Jacob, something new. She felt settled. Secure. Every now and then she would steal glances of him. She loved the way he looked at her, the way he made her feel but most of all she loved the way he was. Calm and commanding. Authoritative but gentle. She looked up at him with large blue eyes. As he met her gaze. She kissed him. "Take me to bed Mr. Rivers" she said smiling. He stood, lifted her from the couch with both arms and carried her up the stairs.

# CHAPTER 11

Charlie Hobbs was born in 1984 to a working-class couple in Longbenton, Newcastle Upon Tyne. Always big for his age, he was frequently in fights throughout school because of his quick temper, but he quickly learned that he could use his size to his advantage. In his teens he tried a variety of fighting disciplines such as boxing, karate and judo. At eighteen he joined the army, serving four years before being dishonourably discharged for insubordination. At twenty-two he became a doorman and slowly became involved in organized crime. Over the years he forged a name for himself for being extremely capable of horrendous violence toward anyone who got in his way. In the early days he became involved in extortion and racketeering before venturing into trafficking and prostitution. Now he was setting up a deal which would potentially flood the entire Northeast with narcotics. He had access and control of countless pubs, bars, clubs and strip clubs and no one to oppose him. He even had the police on his payroll, meaning he could operate with near immunity.

In less than a week Charlie would run the city, within a month the whole region.

•••

It was Tuesday morning. Rebecca had finalized one last report needed on an old case. All loose ends were now tied, and she was ready to dedicate her time fully to 'The Committee' and its aims. She needed to recruit personnel to handle the intelligence side of the business and secure a headquarters to base them in. They would need equipment such as desks, computers, secure servers, and encrypted communications.

She would also need a fleet for their agents with untraceable plates as well as weaponry that was clean and again untraceable. She would lay the foundations first then move on to securing the operatives. That would be easy. They wouldn't refuse because they couldn't. She lit a cigarette and smiled triumphantly. The work had paid off. The project had been a success, and this was just the start. She stopped herself from getting carried away, took a drag of her cigarette and exhaled. "Change is coming" she said.

•••

By Wednesday mid-morning the contractors had been working around the clock, carrying out everything from decorating to furniture and equipment installations - time was of the essence and Rebecca, as was her nature, was suffering no fools.

The contractors had never been so intimidated. Mainly because they did not know how to react. In heels, Rebecca was just above six foot. She was incredibly attractive, with pale skin, brown eyes and a blunt platinum blonde bob. She was thin but had the presence of a military sergeant. She was unwavering and used eye contact like she was wielding a knife. Highly intelligent and statuesque she was indeed formidable.

The office was in disarray but was usable for her needs. She opened her laptop and connected to the secure network. She picked up her phone and sent Grey wolf and Rainbow a joint message which read;

"The Committee is changing. You will be part of that change. You will soon be sent conference information which you will attend via the company sever. You will be present for the update or you will face severe consequences. Please ensure you keep your identities hidden until you have received your orders." Message sent she set up the conference call and sent to each recipient's profile.

She held all the aces, but time was ticking, and she was becoming impatient. She lit a cigarette and surveyed her new home of operation. There was work to be done.

•••

Jacob was in the shop when he got the new message. He took out his phone and looked at the notification. It was from anonymous and the tone was different than normal, so he knew it wasn't from Rainbow. This was from a committee member and that could not bode well. He had a demand to attend by order; this could only be bad news. In all his time with the Committee there had been only one change that was when he was assigned Rainbow as control. Before Rainbow he had a female control by the name of Medusa. She had a raspy voice which Jacob surmised to have been from a life of heavy smoking. The notification that she had been replaced was formal as usual. As was normal in the Committee, no reasons were given in explanation for the change lest someone be able to use that information to identify their colleague. Code names and minimal contact were key to keeping their identities secret. The higher members of the Committee knew all the details of who worked for them of course. Whether they knew it or not each operative was subject to routine surveillance. If an agent were to be caught freelancing as a killer for hire, tipping people off or acting in any way contradictory to the interests of the Committee, they would deal with it swiftly and fatally.

Should an agent wish to leave the Committee they had two options; the easiest way was financial. They had to buy their freedom by paying the committee a fee based on the percentage of jobs they had done. The longer they had been on the books the less they needed to contribute. This acted as an insurance policy (indemnity) to keep agents active for longer and safeguard the Committee against exposure through financial contribution. The second way was death, either at the hands of a target, the Committee or suicide.

•••

Tal had been enjoying an early lunch with Andrew when his phone vibrated. He checked his messages to see a message by anonymous. He had been summoned to a briefing which filled him with excitement. Perhaps his application to be a field operative had progressed, he thought. Maybe a second stage interview? Andrew returned from the bar with their drinks. "Something must be good based on your smile, is it the message or the drinks?" Andrew asked. "Oh, a combination of things" said Tal taking a sip of his mocha. "Life is good, is it not?" He said.

Jacob received the connection details for the conference with the Committee. He had closed the shop and set up in the basement, placing a high-powered lamp behind his seat. With the rest of the room unlit the light would create a silhouette - his laptop camera would show a figure with no discernible features. He opened the audio software he had to alter his voice. With his face obscured by shadow and his voice a good octave lower than normal, he could be anyone. He would be in a holding lounge until the Committee member, as host, began the meeting.

After a few minutes Jacob's screen showed three separate windows. One showing himself as a silhouette, another showing a similar ghost and the other showed a woman, fully lit with a serious expression. She was wearing glasses and a dark suit. "Grey wolf and Rainbow" she said, "Thank you both for being present and punctual. My name is Rebecca Trafford, and I am the architect of the Committee. Amongst my other governmental duties, I have presided over the Committee and all aspects of its functioning. The day has come for change, in that from today, her majesty the Queen and her secret intelligence service, also known as MI6, require our organisation to operate as new branch of fully fledged agents of the crown. As such your duties will continue as directed. You will be granted protection from prosecution on UK soil should you be compromised, however, remember that you are classed as deniable agents. You will have access to untraceable weaponry and vehicles. You will engage in activities as directed whether on domestic or foreign soil as the Crown sees fit. Should you wish to no longer be a part of the Committee; all past works will be counted as criminal activity against you. Amnesty will only be awarded to you in exchange for your, voluntary, acceptance of your new position."

Jacob could barely believe his ears, he noticed Rebecca smirk as she said "Voluntary". It was either join or die.

"Your response gentlemen?" said Rebecca.

"I am in!" said the figure. His voice though scrambled, still understandable.

"Thank you Rainbow. Grey wolf?"

"I accept, of course" said Jacob, peeved by this ultimatum.

"Welcome to her Majesty's Britannic Secret Service" she said. "You will be paired together on an upcoming mission and time is of the essence. It is a high-risk operation; gentlemen make no mistakes. You will both need to become acquainted beforehand. I have taken the liberty of issuing you with a time and place. Following that you will be contacted with information regarding the location of arms and transport." she said and with that the conference was terminated.

Jacob's phone buzzed, the new message said: Piccadilly Gardens. Thirty minutes. Take something blue for identification.

Jacob left immediately. As usual, he wanted to be early to stake out the area. He had no reason to doubt the Committee or suspect an ambush, but he was meticulous. He certainly was not about to leave anything to chance. Piccadilly Gardens is an open green space in the centre of Manchester surrounded by a mix of historic and modern architecture. There is a large, curved wall which runs along one side of the gardens which provides access to the bus terminal. The wall itself has the look of something you might expect to find in a former eastern bloc country.

Jacob sat in the top section of a McDonalds which gave a great view of the whole area. He hated the smell of the food in the air, he felt like it was forming a layer of grease on his clothes and hair, but he would have no issue seeing the mystery colleague arrive from here. Just then he saw a familiar face in the crowd. He was trying to blend in, but Jacob could see his movements were for reconnaissance. Jacob watched him circle the gardens before picking a spot where his back was to the wall but, if needed, he could slip through the middle opening to the bus terminal. Jacob watched as the gentleman pulled out a blue pocket square from his coat and began handling it as if to be folding his accessory. His heart stopped for a brief second. "You have got to be kidding" he said to himself with a grin.

Jacob left the restaurant and made his way across to join his old friend. On his approach, Tal still surveying the area caught his eye. "Jacob!" he said not expecting to see him in the middle of a rendezvous. "Are you waiting for someone?" asked Jacob calmly, toying with Tal, who was noticeably nervous over the prospect of having a plus one at his first secret service meeting.

"Jacob my boy, yes, sorry I have a meeting with…."

"With someone holding something blue" Jacob finished for him.

Tal went to speak before realising Jacob was who he was waiting on.

"Dear god! My boy, no!" Tal said clapping and flashing one of his incredible smiles.

"let us head to the shop" said Jacob "I think we have a lot to discuss". With that they made their way back to Knightsbridge.

Back at the shop Jacob pulled the light switch and the two agents descended the wooden staircase to the basement. Jacob pulled out a stool and motioned for Tal to take a seat before taking two glasses and a bottle of Woodford reserve bourbon from a cabinet. "We may need this" he said placing the items on the table.

He poured them both a generous measure. They raised their glasses to each other and took a sip, both men pursing their lips as the fire made its way down their throats.

"So, how in the world did Talib Abayoe end up here?" asked Jacob.

"Well," began Tal, "You know of my coming to the United Kingdom from Sudan as an orphan and refugee?"

"Yes" said Jacob.

"Before I arrived, I had spent two years along with tens of thousands of others as a child soldier. My parents were killed by the army and my sisters were taken as wives. So, from an early age I wanted to help to serve justice in some way. Not through the judiciary system, as, in my experience, rich and powerful men do not go to jail. When I arrived in England, I saw other people in positions of authority carrying out despicable acts. These people would not answer to anyone for their crimes. In one such instance in my late teens, a friend of mine had been beaten and raped. The police came to see her in hospital to ask questions. She said it was a group of four men. They had tricked her into thinking she was auditioning for a model agency. This group dealt in trafficking and prostitution and were known to the police; however, they could not prove it was them on this occasion. When she died two days later from her injuries, I went to the police station. There a senior officer told me of a Committee that might be able to offer some assistance. As I could not afford the bounty, I did what I could to be a part of their solution. Here I am. What is your storey? Art dealer?" said Tal with a smile.

Jacob took another sip. "When I was seven; someone broke into our home around Christmas. My mother and father were both stabbed when they intervened. It was not an act of desperation. He stabbed them both a total of nearly forty times. I later found out that this same person had gone on the run. The police had no way of locating him. In any case, I went into care and that was that. Until years later as an adult, I saw an article about a family found around Christmas who had been fatally stabbed with all the familiar hallmarks. My old friend as it happened was a serial killer. A person in the know referred me to an organisation that might help. So, I contacted the Committee who said they could not accept the task as they could not confirm crimes to be verified. Like you Tal, I needed justice. I could not let it lie so I told them I would do it myself. I would track him down, make him confess and end him." Jacob took another drink. "So, I did just that. I recorded his confession and I played it over the phone to the Committee when it was all over. I told them of all the lives this man had taken and that without my involvement he would still be free. I am not sure why, but I felt the need to let them know what they had missed. As it happens, they had me under surveillance the whole time and it appeared they liked my work. The whole thing was a bizarre job interview."

Tal raised a glass and said, "And here we are, small world my boy."

Jacob smiled and said, "you know, I'm actually pleased it is you."

"Yes, me too my boy" said Tal.

Jacob fired up his laptop and logged on to the server. The display had changed. Now instead of a single folder on a black screen there was a host links running along the top of the screen. There was a mail icon, a task folder, Government surveillance, ANPR, satellite imagery. The mail and task icons had an alert to show something was new. Jacob turned the screen so that Tal could see, double clicking- he opened the mail icon. There was a single email which read.

"Deansgate car park. Black Audi Q7. Reg: R933 LTE. Tinted windows. Keys under rear wheel arch. Tools are provided in a locked case in the boot. Code for case is 79823."

"Looks like we have wheels" Tal remarked.

"Yes, but where will they be taking us?" replied Jacob moving his cursor to the task Icon. Clicking that link brought up a page with tabs along the bottom. This document had a cover page with subsequent information on places, people and arms.

"What have we gotten ourselves into?" asked Tal as the two of them looked through the document.

"Says here that there is a time limit to this one. There is a deal happening the day after tomorrow which is when we need to be in a position to eradicate this target and his crew." Said Jacob, adding "by the looks of it they are numerous, heavily armed and dangerous including some ex-military" rubbing his chin in contemplation.

"So, what now? Two men on a suicide mission to end a drug cartel?" said Tal rubbing the back of his neck and exhaling.

"We need to get that car and see what we have to work with. If we do not comply, we will spend the rest of our lives in jail or running." Said Jacob looking at Tal.

"We need to know, aside from her majesty's pleasure what is in it for us other than being at odds with the secret service." Said Tal.

"That's a good point." Said Jacob "That's a very good point."

# CHAPTER 12

Ten minutes later Jacob and Tal were in the car park scanning the rows of parked cars for one that matched the description. Parked in a dimly lit corner they found their transport. Jacob reached under the left rear wheel arch. Nothing. He moved around to the right rear side of the vehicle and ran his hand up under the arch where he found the keys taped to the inside of the upper rim. He pulled the tape from the keys and pressed the unlock button on the fob to open the boot. There as expected was a weapons case. Tal noted the combination lock and said, "if I am not mistaken the code was 79823" and he spun the numbers until he heard the unmistakable click of the lock disengaging. Tal shot Jacob a glance they felt a childlike anticipation before gingerly opening the lid. The two of them stared in amazement; it was like Christmas had come early. The case contained a variety or arms such as a Sig SG540 rifle capable of a range of 800 meters that can be used in conjunction with sight and bipod to become an effective sniper rifle. There was an M4 Carbine, a Winchester 12 Defender 6 round shot gun, a Heckler & Koch HK416. As for handguns there was a Star 30M which held fifteen rounds and a Glock 20 which caught Jacobs' eye.

"I know what I want" said Jacob as he pointed to the Glock, the Sig and the HK416. "Jacob my boy, that's absolutely fine with me. We share similar tastes in art but not in arms it appears." To the side of the crate Were two bullet proof vests, some long-range radio communications equipment and a bag containing six stun grenades and a set of fake number plates. Lastly there were two document wallets. One for Jacob and one for Tal. Inside each contained false identities by way of documentation such as passports, driver's licences and ID's.

The quality of weapons was not lost on the pair, they knew this meant they would be going to war and would need to be prepared. Particularly as they had precious little time for surveillance and planning. They would need to go in decisively and tactically as they would be outnumbered. They would have to create an advantage.

They drove their newly acquired arsenal back to Jacob's house, where they had agreed they would study their brief that evening and make an early start the next day. The more time they would have to prepare the better. On the drive back to Wilmslow he called Laura.

"Hey, how are you doing?" she asked.

"I'm fine, Listen, I have to attend a last-minute exhibition so I will be away for a day or two" he said. He hated not being able to tell her the truth.

"Oh ok, pity I have so much work on or I could have joined you" she said. Under normal circumstances he would have loved that. "I know but it's only for a couple of nights, I will call you as soon as I am on my way back and we can go out somewhere?" he said.

"That would be great Mr. Rivers. Are you ok, you sound a little stressed?" she said. "Yeah, this thing has just come out of nowhere, really important though." He said, hating every minute that he could not be honest with her. "Ok well, until then, keep out of trouble" she said. "I will try but I cannot promise. Until then" he said. "Until then" she replied and with that the call ended. Personal life now on hold, Jacob steeled himself for the task ahead. He had to be focused. Failure to keep his head could cost him his life.

Back home he studied the report. Charlie and his team were supposed to be meeting a team of Czech mafia on the Gateshead quayside near the Baltic Flour Mill at the Mill Road car park 8pm. There would be an exchange of money for a substantial supply of drugs. The informant had added to the report that Charlie would likely take two cars. There would be eight men, including Charlie, and they would be armed. Only three of them, however, had military training. Once the deal was done, Charlie's plan was to head to the other side of the Tyne bridge to begin distributing immediately in time for Friday night. In bold red text at the bottom the report stated, TARGET CANNOT BE KILLED PRIOR TO THE EXCHANGE. It would be the last act to justify his elimination.

Jacob brought up a 3D map of the area on his laptop to see what other buildings; vantage points and cover were available. He had been to the Baltic Flour Mill once before shortly after it opened as a gallery, but he needed to refresh his memory of the area.
He noted the route toward Newcastle via the Tyne bridge was mostly a one-way system, which could come in handy. He continued to commit the profiles and landscape to memory. "If only Tal could bloody drive!" he thought. He would have to position him early on. This was problematic on two fronts. Jacob had until now, always worked alone. Now he needed to position an accomplice but also one that would need assistance with transport if they needed to move.

He would need to factor in rendezvous points if they were to strike in multiple places.

It was getting late. He needed to pack, arrange accommodation and get a good night sleep, which would be easier said than done. He felt a pang of regret that he had not left the Committee when the thought crossed his mind. Now he was trapped, he had no choice. His thoughts began to gather "How was he going to continue in this double life? If Laura knew how would she react? Maybe he could keep it hidden but how?". "One problem at a time" he sighed. "I will worry about that if I survive".

Tal had also been hard at work studying the area and documents to get as much information as possible. He made mental notes as to which of the targets would have the most experience and therefore be more of a threat. He knew Jacob would be calling the shots as he was the senior operative being experienced in this field of work, but he wanted to prove himself to be just as capable. This was no time for egos of course, both needed to be synchronised. As the old saying goes "A stupid friend is more dangerous than an enemy" and if both were to survive, neither had time to be foolish. Satisfied he could learn no more he shut down his laptop and looked out of his window to the city below.

# CHAPTER 13

The next day, Jacob had been waiting for Tal in the layby outside Beetham tower. While he waited, he tried to distract himself looking at the features of his new company car. It had been a strange morning. Jacob had woken with a terrible feeling in his stomach. He couldn't place it. It wasn't nervousness for the task ahead. He kept thinking about Laura. He replayed the memory of how she looked at the exhibition, and later back at his house. He remembered carrying her up the stairs to the bedroom and helping her undress. How they had kissed. The look in her eyes; how soft her skin was, the smell of her hair and the night they had shared. He also thought of the morning after, how softly she had slept beside him and how badly he wanted that to be a daily occurrence.

Just then Tal appeared at the main doors carrying a small overnight case. He was wearing skinny fit grey trousers, and an oversized black shirt and beanie hat with his trusty loafers. He stored his case on the back seat before climbing inside the front next to Jacob. "Good morning my boy" he said. Jacob was a little saddened to not see the usual bright beaming smile. "How are you?" asked Jacob, concerned.
"Prepared, ready and under no illusions that this is not the movies." Said Tal.
Jacob was reassured to hear this. He placed a hand on Tal's shoulder and said "If we take care of each other, work as a team, we will succeed. Remember, this is not some mercenary, senseless killing. This is official -Crown approved." Jacob pinched his fingers at the

bridge of his nose and said, "How in the bloody hell did we end up as secret agents?" He began to laugh at how absurd the reality of the situation was. Tal turned to him and grinned before joining him in laughing.

Jacob put the car in gear and started off.

Jacob had been pleased to hear Tal speak so resolutely and with such focus. It wasn't like it was in the movies, here the hero throws bodies out of the way dispatching bad guy after bad guy without remorse or a flicker of emotion. Truth be told, each of the cases Jacob had worked had affected him - despite the targets being more than deserving. If you were not affected it could only mean one thing, that you had strayed over the line and become one of them. This was not done to satisfy a personal kink or pleasure. This was *not* done to feel dominance, perverted arousal or to fulfil some warped fantasy. This was done in the name of justice, cold revenge for those who had been wronged. An old testament, eye for an eye to re-adjust the balance. The only pleasure Jacob received from each of his past assignments was the thought of delivering peace or closure to the family of those in need of his services.

The traffic was lighter once they got on the motorway heading north-east on the A1, the only hindrance was the fifty-mile an hour zones for road works and narrow lanes which seemed to go on for ever. Tal and Jacob discussed the information they had both learnt on their target and his crew, the weapons they would make use of and other tactics to force separation firstly from the Czechs then dividing Charlie's team. Although the numbers were against them, with careful planning and the element of surprise they had a fair chance of success. Of course, they would survey the area once they arrived to ensure nothing would compromise their vantage points. They would also need to check they were out of the line of sight of any CCTV cameras, particularly since the handover was taking place in a public carpark. They needed to be careful - it was unfamiliar ground on a Friday night. Newcastle was known for its nightlife which meant the possibility of running into bystanders which could double up as witnesses or potential collateral damage neither of which would be ideal.

Five minutes from their destination, Jacob woke Tal who had been asleep for the past hour. They were booked in at the Ramada Encore hotel on the Gateshead Quayside just a few minutes away from the strike location. Jacob had arranged for two single rooms under false names. The concierge had been chatty during the booking, so Jacob had been careful not to offer too much information. He had been polite but unremarkable. Just another client visiting for a stag do perhaps. Jacob pulled into the carpark, he made a point of not parking too close to the main doors, not that their car was particularly recognisable, but he wanted it to be lost in the sea of other vehicles. Securely parked, Jacob and Tal both collected their luggage from the boot. Aside from their cases containing clothing they each had a duffle bag containing their weapons, ammunition, vests and communication equipment. They walked through the entrance to the check-in desk where they were greeted by a thin young man with bleach blonde hair, a navy-blue suit and a lilac shirt. The interior was modern and was decorated with an overly red theme. The reception desk, the wall behind it and the walls leading to the waiting lounge and the sofas and chairs were all red with criss-crossed white strip lights overhead. Tal scanned the room and said, "My boy, do you think they got a discount by sticking to one colour?" Jacob surveyed the entrance hall. "It is certainly red" said Jacob with a grimace. At that moment, the concierge looked up from his administration work. "Afternoon gentlemen. Do you have a booking with us?" he asked looking them both over. "Yes, we do." Said Jacob "Barnes and Forbes." The hotel worker clicked his mouse, typed in the names and read his computer screen "Ah, yes here we are." He said. He fished around the desk before placing two keys on the countertop. "Rooms 314 and 315. Please follow the corridor to the right toward the lifts. Dinner is served between 7pm and 8:30pm and breakfast is from 6:30am to 8:30am." Tal and Jacob collected their keys and nodded in appreciation and made their way toward the lifts. The small lift was a tight squeeze with their luggage which was a curious design flaw given that people who frequent hotels often carry bags and are not always likely to take the stairs with them. Arriving at the third floor, the doors slid open and they were met with another red wall in the corridor. Tal groaned, "I wonder how angry the interior designer was when they picked the colour scheme?" he said making Jacob laugh. They continued to their rooms, "I wonder what we will find in here" said Jacob said opening the door. He was met with a modest size room, wooden floors, desk and headboard. The bed was a good size although the base and runner were – as expected – red, as were the curtains, the desk chair and the corner sofa. Jacob could not help but chuckle overhearing Tal in the adjacent room exclaim, "Are you kidding me?"

Once their belongings were secured in their rooms, Tal and Jacob made their way out toward the Baltic Flour Mill and the carpark for a recce. The sky overhead was steel grey with a strong breeze and a light drizzle began to fall. "We have the element of surprise; we just need a way to remove the Czechs and then the leader from the pack" Said Jacob taking in the scene.

The carpark had one road leading in and out to the south which was accompanied by a tree line. To the north it was tiered, with steps leading down two levels to the quayside and millennium bridge. It was framed by the distinctive Sage to the west and the Baltic flour mill and apartments to the east.

The only clear vantage point to snipe from an elevated position was the Baltic-Quay apartments however, this meant if things went sour, Tal would be on the ground alone with potentially all eight targets. By the time Jacob would make it down to ground level it would be too late.

The tiered levels and tree line could offer some cover from return fire, however, and keep them out of sight of bystanders. There was a fence surrounding the carpark which meant the stairs were the only route available on foot, which narrowed the options for a target to escape whilst under fire. Their only way to relative safety while on foot from the carpark would be down the stairs toward the quayside and over the bridge. They would have to scare away the Czechs and disable Charlie's vehicles so that he and his mob were stranded on foot. While Jacob lead with fire from the tree line cover, Tal could head off the fleeing members if he set up on the tier below, picking them off as they descended. If they left the car on the lower tier which was accessed by the road beside the river, they could work their way down and away from the scene. It was risky, but it could work.

•••

That evening Tal and Jacob spent time in their rooms in preparation. Stripping down and cleaning rifles and pistols, sharpening knives and preparing their minds. Both were nervous. For Jacob, this was an abnormal situation. He hadn't worked with someone on a job before and, though he did not question Tal's ability, he would be reliant on an accomplice to act and make decisions that would not only affect the outcome of their objective but also had the potential to cost them their lives. This gave him cause for concern. If only they had been able to carry out training together to synchronise their processes he thought. He finished reassembling his arms and checking them over, ensuring they were clean and functioning perfectly before returning them to the holdall at the end of his bed. He looked out the window surveying the scene. After a few minutes he lay on the bed supporting his head with a folded arm and thought about Laura. He wasn't used to this either. He wondered what she might be doing and whether there would be any future chance of explaining this part of his life. He cast his mind back to the exhibition, he remembered the look on her face, the way she moved, how happy she had been. Just then a knock at the door stole him from his reverie. "My boy! Let's eat" said Tal from the corridor. At that moment Jacob realised how hungry he was. He lifted himself off the bed and rubbed his face with his hands exhaling slowly. He turned to look back at the holdall as if expecting reassurance. They would be outnumbered, outgunned and not fully prepared. He closed his eyes for a second and breathed deeply before leaving the room to join Tal.


The Millennium bridge offered an iconic view. Against the darkening sky stood the silhouette of both the Tyne bridge and the High-level bridge. The buildings on either side adding a majestic air as their lights reflected across the water. As night drew in Jacob and Tal crossed the bridge. They both walked with their hands in their coat pockets as a cold drizzle began to fall. Looking to Jacob, Tal cocked his head, narrowed his eyebrows and said, "My boy, you do not seem your usual cheery self, what's troubling you?" Thinking for a moment before answering, Jacob replied, "For a second I thought I was in control" he said looking back at Tal. "I thought I had some idea of what I was doing."

Tal nodded and ran his tongue across his bottom lip in consideration before adding "I take it this is not task related, more a matter of the heart?"

They both came to a stop and faced each other. Jacob shrugged his shoulders then said, "I know, I'm acting like a bloody schoolboy. Melancholy and distracted when we have more important matters to focus on."

Tal raised a hand and placed it on Jacobs shoulder and said, "Without the ability to feel compassion or affection we would be nothing more than ruthless killers. What would we be trying to achieve, doing what we do if it were not out of justice and compassion? You deserve happiness as much as the people we work on behalf of. I am sure it will work out for you and the delightful Laura."

Jacob smiled and patted Tal on the arm. "Let us get some food before we get soaked through eh?"

Not long after, Jacob and Tal were settling into their seats. They didn't want to stray too far from the hotel and risk being caught by any cameras or get involved in any altercations or situations whereby they may be remembered. The bar was called the pitcher and piano, which was a glass fronted building with great visibility of river and the footfall around the area. The service was friendly their food and drinks were in front of them in no time at all.

"They speak so strangely here" said Tal, sipping a gin cocktail. "But they certainly know how to have fun; this is my kind of city".

Jacob laughed and reached for his bottle of beer, "So, were all clear on tomorrow?" he asked.

"All clear" said Tal making eye contact, and they clinked their drinks together.

Over dinner they discussed art, film and music and shared stories of travel and experiences. They were careful not to over-indulge with alcohol, but a few drinks allowed them to relax. Fed and unwound from the day, the two men headed back over the bridge to where they were relieved to see the concierge desk was vacant, meaning they could avoid small talk. The less people that saw them the less people could identify them. In their line of work anonymity was a superpower.

Bidding each other a good night they returned to their separate rooms to see what sleep might come their way. Jacob spent some time stretching before reading for a short while. Tal on the other hand was sound asleep as soon as his head hit the pillow.

•••

Terri was having difficulty sleeping. He was restless and the hospice bed was uncomfortable. No matter how he shifted he simply could not settle. He sat in the dark looking up toward the ceiling as thoughts came and went. He knew time wasn't on his side and his thoughts turned to death. Not his death but the death of a young girl years ago. Terri, Charlie and two other associates had been out drinking since 10am. They had spent the day going from bars to casinos to strip clubs. It was a celebration for a deal they had recently made which gave them significant clout in the region. The empire was growing and seemed unstoppable. It had been a great day which carried on to the night. Terri remembered the four of them in the VIP area of some trendy night club. The girls, he remembered, they were everywhere. Dancing, wearing next to nothing. But Charlie was interested in one girl in particular, a hostess whose job was taking regular orders from the tables and delivering the drinks. She was beautiful, mixed race, young with an amazing body. In contrast to the flesh on display like meat in a butcher's shop window, she had an air or sophistication about her, of class even. Over the course of the night Charlie would whisper into her ear and flash his best smile. She in turn would act coy, touching his arm or playing with her hair. The night wore on and by the time they came to leave Terri was a state but with it enough to remember what happened next. They left the club just after midnight, with the young waitress. The boys laughed as they made their way to a flat Charlie owned nearby. All the while the young lady walked arm in arm with Charlie who looked like a giant next to her. Back at the flat they all enjoyed more drinks. Charlie and the young girl disappeared to his bedroom around 1am while Terri and the other two passed out in the living room.

The next morning Terri woke up feeling terrible only to feel worse moments later. "Terri!" Charlie shouted – he sounded panicked. "Yeah, what is it Charlie?" he said as he heaved himself from the sofa. "I need a favour mate." Said Charlie motioning with his head toward the bedroom. Charlie stood in the doorway fully clothed. He must have been up early, thought Terri. He made his way to the bedroom door where Charlie ushered him in. That is when he sobered up. There tangled in the sheets was the young girl. She looked as though she had been hit by a train. "Charlie, what the …." He trailed off unable to turn away from the sight before him. Charlie sniffed, "Was going great until she got all moral and said no, been telling her all night I'd make her a model, I told her I'd make her rich. She slapped me saying she was not a whore. After that, well she didn't put up a fight."

Terri, felt sick, he remembered how lively she was last night and to see her now was a stark reminder of who his master was and what he was capable of.

"I'll get rid of her Charlie" Said Terri, aware of what a low life he had become.

A week later he had called the hospital as a concerned passer-by, after initially being told that they could not give out any information to strangers, his past police negotiation skills worked wonders and he managed to sweet talk the receptionist. He found out that she had passed away from her injuries. It was at that point; Terri knew Charlie had to be stopped but that he was too much a coward to do it himself. He lay in the dark, staring at the ceiling, eyes filling with tears of shame, convinced the devil was in the room counting down the days to claim his soul.

•••

It had been an eventful and tiring few days and Laura was looking forward to spending some time to herself. She was feeling incredibly pleased though. Thanks to the recent sales she had a healthy bank balance and, further to that, she was receiving offers from magazines for work. She decided to surprise Jacob when he returned from his job up north - she planned on making a fuss of him. She packed a bag and went to stay at his house - he had given her a key and had insisted that she make herself at home after all. Their relationship had been moving rather quickly but it was comfortable, natural even. "Why should a relationship be measured by some fictional time frame anyway?" she had thought. She sat on his luxurious sofa updating her website with her latest work and adding descriptions to her gallery. Looking up from her laptop she reached over to the table and picked up her cup of coffee. She held it in both hands feeling the warmth creep through her fingers. "Mrs Laura Rivers" she said out loud before smiling to herself.

# CHAPTER 14

It had taken years of working diligently within the secret service before Rebecca Trafford was able to present her proposal. The aim of the project was simple: justice. In the United Kingdom, Criminal courts decided the outcome of a trial based on the burden of proof; being that someone is deemed guilty beyond all reasonable doubt. Additional factors may be presented such as physical evidence, alibi and motive but these can be manipulated to either liberate or condemn a person depending on the persuasiveness of the argument. There is an outstanding amount of wrongful convictions as well as acquittals - a good lawyer can convince a jury, beyond reasonable doubt that a defendant is either guilty or not simply by presenting facts in a certain light. Justice then, is ultimately subjective to the power of argument and, as such, how can it be truly just?

Such was the case almost forty years ago now. They had been out for the day to an amusement park to celebrate their little girl turning eight. Richard and Catherine were so proud of their only child. She excelled in school and was so wise beyond her few years that sometimes they wondered if they had a child prodigy on their hands. They had left early that morning to make good time and avoid traffic and queues for tickets. Whilst there they enjoyed all the rides Rebecca was tall enough to ride and for lunch, she was treated to fast food which was a true rarity. After a wonderful day they returned to their car and made the journey home. They sang along to the radio happily until eventually, exhausted, Rebecca fell asleep in the back seat. Richard and Catherine recounted their highlights of the day in hushed tones and discussed their plans for the following week. They were planning on getting a family pet as a late surprise; however, that would never happen because the world, unfortunately, is not a fair place.

A little after 6:30pm, Chris Duffy left the White lion pub. He had been drinking for nearly five hours since finishing his early shift around 1pm. He only lived a few miles from the pub, and he had driven home in worse states plenty of times before. Putting the car into 1st gear he pulled out of the pub car park.

Rebecca woke in agony. There were flashing lights and strange noises, but she could not make out what they were. The world was upside down and strange silhouettes moved around her speaking in a language she could not seem to understand. Slowly her vision faded, sounds evaporated and everything became nothing.

Rebecca remained in hospital for over a month. She had suffered multiple breaks and fractures but was recovering well physically. Mentally, however, she was scarred. She had not recovered enough to attend the funeral of her parents and would be living with her grandmother from now on. For all the sympathetic words and pitying looks from the nurses, police and other visitors, her world had been damaged beyond repair.

It was only due to sheer determination that Rebecca forced her grandmother to let her attend the trial. Despite her years Rebecca understood what was happening. Her grandmother had explained it as best she could; both sides were telling their version of the story and the people sat at the side of the court in their little box on the benches would decide which version they believed. Rebecca noticed that the man in charge of representing her family was a very sweaty man who also looked very tired. He mumbled and fumbled with bits of paper and looked very unkempt. The bad man's lawyer was dressed very smartly and was very loud. He reminded Rebecca of a TV presenter. He would smile a lot and gesture dramatically with his arms and he kept the attention of the people in the box every time he spoke. He would sometimes make fun of the sweaty man and make the people laugh which made the judge hit a hammer on his desk and say "Order!"

Chris Duffy spent just six months in prison for drunk driving. The truth was that he murdered two people by driving head on into oncoming traffic. His selfish actions had robbed a little girl of her family, her childhood and destroyed the very construct of her world. But, because Chris Duffy's lawyer was able to articulate his argument better than the Trafford's lawyer who was on the verge of a breakdown at the time, the jury felt that he was not guilty of manslaughter merely driving whilst under the influence. This, apparently, was justice served.

Rebecca was determined to change the system. She argued that the money invested in offenders such as these did not lead to rehabilitation. The system could be manipulated far too easily with bribes, concealed evidence, fabricated or planted evidence, intimidation, misinformation, red tape, politics and diplomatic immunity.

Parameters would be needed of course, processes. A burden of proof or standard for conviction. Like the smartly dressed lawyer years ago, she received support from her seniors by way of a convincing argument. Justice beyond the courts. There were conditions, it would have to be kept under the radar and be proven beneficial for the country of course and subject to a trial period. They would be known as "The Committee" and they would preside over all applications of justice or injustice as it were.

Of course, the fact that Chris Duffy was first on the list was overlooked. After all, true justice is subjective to the offended.

# CHAPTER 15

Friday morning. Jacob and Tal were up early. Fortune shone on them once more as they went to checkout, the concierge was nowhere to be seen. They dropped their keys off on the desk and headed out to the car. "We'll have to park the car, so we're guaranteed a space later" said Jacob. Opening the boot, Jacob took out and attached the set of false Number plates while Tal kept an eye out. Fake plates secured, they drove round to the parking area, purchased a day ticket to eliminate the risk of a ticket. Later they would return for the weapons roughly an hour before the rendezvous and set up. First, they would have to endure the worst part of the job…waiting.

Night was drawing in. Jacob was in position concealed in the hedges at the entrance to the car park. He and Tal were in communication thanks to the comms link provided by their new employer. Armed with the Heckler & Koch HK416, Glock pistol and knife. He lay on the ground, relaxed. The rifle barrel was resting on his left forearm while his right hand held the gun upright. Every now and again he looked through the scope, checking distances, readying himself.

Meanwhile, Tal was based on the lower tier. He was armed only with his Star 30M pistol which was holstered under his coat and a couple of flash bang grenades in each coat pocket. He carried a coffee and wore a beanie hat not only to keep warm but also to provide a disguise. The plan was simple, it had to be given their lack time for them to prepare. Jacob would open fire in a bid to disable Charlie's vehicles and ground his team – the Czechs would be allowed to flee the scene. Tal would then add to the confusion by using the Stun grenades from the rear position to disorientate Charlie's mob, giving Jacob time to get to his feet and sweep in with his pistol, taking out targets and driving any fleeing survivors towards Tal. Tal could then pick the remaining men off as they descended the stairs. They had to be precise, they had to be swift, and they had to be aggressive.

Tal called Jacob via the comms link. "How is the view, Grey wolf?" Jacob replied, "All clear for now, will update when the situation changes". The tension was awful, like an Olympic sprinter poised in the stocks waiting for the starting gun, both Tal and Jacob doing their best to stay calm and relaxed.

It was 7:45pm; the area was mostly quiet with only a few joggers, lost in their own worlds, passing by Tal along the quayside path. The sun was setting and the day giving way to dusk. Tal checked his watch - it was almost time. He stood with his back to the wall beside the stairs and out of site from the carparks elevated position. "In position, Grey wolf." He said over the comms link. "Copy that." Jacob responded. It felt as if time had stood still, if it were not for the movement of the river below Jacob could have sworn time had stopped.

And then, suddenly, "We have action, repeat action, two cars on approach!" reported Jacob. "Welcome to the party, Charlie" said Tal standing up straight, hands buried in his pockets ready for the signal. Charlie's two cars slowly drove into the car park coming to a stop left of the middle and parking one slightly forward of the other diagonally. Not ideal thought Jacob however, there was enough space between them to see both drivers and both front tyres, although it would offer cover on the passenger side. Through the scope he could see that there were only five men. Two in the forward car and three in the rear car, one of which was Charlie. "Five, including the target confirmed." Said Jacob to alert Tal to the situation. This was looking better, so far, the intel was near enough correct and the numbers were more favourable. However, it was likely Charlie had dropped off some of his men at the top of the road to cut off the Czechs if things went south. If that were the case, then this had potential to go even better. A third car made its way into the carpark, a black SUV with tinted windows making it difficult to identify how many people were in the car. Slowly it rolled to a stop a few meters from the other two cars. Charlie and his two fellow passengers stepped out of their cars. They closed the doors and waited, while the two drivers stayed in their cars, engines off but lights left on. The passenger doors of the SUV opened in unison and three military looking men stepped out, one with a large bag. The driver of the SUV remained behind the wheel. "Be ready…" Jacob Whispered.

Charlie and his thugs strode slowly toward the Czechs. Through his scope Jacob saw what a mountain of a man Charlie was, he was flanked by a shorter stocky man with dark hair and a taller bald man who carried the money. "It only means more target area" he thought. Charlie briefly shook hands with the man carrying the bag and they talked for a minute or two, both using wide arm gestures, posturing. The leather of Jacobs's gloves made a creaking sound as he adjusted his position, taking long slow breaths. "Any minute now…" Charlie motioned to the man on his right who was carrying a duffle bag who moved forward and exchanged it with the Czech, in doing so he had unknowingly blocked Jacob's direct line of sight on Charlie. "Trade has been made, here we go…" Jacob said and opened fire.

It took seconds for Charlie and his men to understand what was happening, as bullets whipped past them into the tyres and engines of their two cars. The Czech's were more on the ball and spun on their heels and darted to their vehicle, keeping low as they went. Charlie and his two companions ducked and dashed for the cover of their cars, each of them shouting over each other. Front tyres now ruined; Jacob raised his aim. Through the scope he caught the expression of the lead driver who was closest to the fleeing targets. The drivers' eyes were wide with panic and his mouth dropped open, he had momentarily frozen in his tracks. Charlie and his thugs watched as a red arc of blood decorated the windshield. There was a screeching of tyres as the Czechs sped away towards the exit. Still composed, Jacob now focused on the remaining driver who was trying to get the car to move on the rims of the ruined wheels in a bid to escape. Jacob calmly squeezed the trigger, and another Jackson Pollock splatter painting adorned the windshield. Vehicles disabled it was time to take out the remaining three men.

Gaining speed, the Czech's SUV made its way out of the car park and toward the main road. "What the fuck was that?" shouted the driver. "Ambush, they must be trying to take the drugs and the money!" shouted the man who had held the bag. The junction to the main road was coming into view about 50 yards ahead. "Bastards don't know who they are fucking with!" 40 yards, "They'll pay for this…" 20 yards and two men stepped out of the bushes on either side of the road, pistols raised and opening fire. Charlie had indeed dropped two of his men as Jacob had thought. "Look ou-…" before he could finish the driver was hit with two fatal shots. The SUV continued passed the junction out of control and over the road, crashing into a factory wall. Charlie's two men swiftly followed to finish off the survivors.

In the carpark, Charlie and his two thugs were trying to take cover behind their cars. They didn't know where the gunfire was coming from, but they knew they wouldn't live long standing out in the open. "Stay behind the cars!" shouted Charlie, "The bastards not having me!"
"Charlie, the cars are fucked!" screamed the bald henchmen, pulling out his gun with one hand the bag of drugs in his other.
For the moment, they were relatively safe but breathing hard and with adrenaline kicking in - it was the urge to fight or flee.
"I'm gonna kill who ever this is!" spat Charlie.
The shorter man raised his head to peer through the car windows to see if he could tell where the gunfire was coming from and said, "D'ya think it's them Czech bastards"
"Aye!" said the bald man
"Lads on the hill will deal with them!" said Charlie, "let's kill this bastard whoever it is!"

Just then everything went bright white. There was a high-pitched ringing in their ears…then silence…and light

Tal had launched three stun grenades in quick succession, each landing in close enough range to be effective. Charlie and the two henchmen were temporarily blinded and deafened. Leaving the HK416 and its spent magazine behind, Jacob ran swiftly toward the cowering and stunned targets, his Glock pistol in hand, aimed and ready.

Tal also had his pistol in his right hand but concealed within folded arms. A few people had stopped to see what the commotion coming from the car park was, but they soon dispersed when the sound of gunfire began again.

Jacob crouched low. He couldn't see the three targets, but they were firing blindly. He returned a few shots to keep them from advancing, he had to keep them where they were or drive them to Tal.

Just then Jacob glimpsed the top of the dark-haired man's head through the car windows, and, in a split second, he aimed and fired.

Shattered glass rained down over the assailant - he had managed to duck in time. The bald man took the initiative and fired off several rounds which flew past Jacob, close enough for him to hear them whiz by. Charlie followed up with a volley. The three men were beginning to regain their senses.

"Fuck this!" said the dark-haired man and he made a run for the lower tier.

"Daz you prick!" shouted the bald man before flinching at the near placed shots from the unknown attacker.

Charlie was fuming, the deal gone sour, he was under fire and Daz had shown himself, when it mattered the most, to be a spineless coward.

Further up the road, Charlie's men approached the SUV cautiously. They knew they won't have killed all its occupants and they had no idea what fire power the Czechs might have.

As they drew nearer each man had their sights on the doors of the vehicle, ready for any movement. They crept closer on either side. The Czechs had the advantage, there were three of them with serious fire power and tinted windows giving them perfect vision from the inside and shielding their movements. Weapons cocked, locked and loaded they let rip from inside the car. Glass exploded as both of Charlie's men took multiple hits at short range. Their bodies fell lifeless to the ground as the Czechs poured from the SUV. One of them took the initiative and blocked the path of an approaching car, his gun aimed at the driver. "Out! Out!" he screamed. The driver, a young male and his girlfriend quickly got out and ran from their small Peugeot 206.

"Get in! Go! Go" the Czechs shouted before making their getaway.

Jacob was now at the rear of the furthest car, he knew the assailants were close, as he crept round the vehicle, he caught sight of the bald man who had seen him advancing too. The two raised their guns and fired simultaneously. To their equal disappointment both clicked redundantly - empty chambers. As the bald thug lunged towards him, Jacob instinctively threw his pistol at him, catching him above the right eye. It stalled him momentarily, giving Jacob the valuable time to retrieve his knife.

Out of nowhere a squat brown-haired man with a gun in his hand rounded the top of the stairs slamming into the railing. He was in a panic and moving faster than his legs could carry him. By the time he had stumbled to the bottom he had absolutely no idea there was another gun on him. Turning his head, he was surprised to see Tal, arm outstretched, weapon brandished.
He stopped in his tracks and opened his mouth as if to say something, but no words emerged. He saw death before him, in a form he would never have expected. Without any delay, Tal fired and ended his life.

The bald man recoiled from the impact of Jacobs's gun and in doing so dropped his own empty weapon. As Jacob rounded the car the other man made a run for it, again in Tal's direction. The plan was working. It had been less than a few minutes since the first shot but, if it went on much longer, they risked police interference. Jacob watched as the bald man made his escape but, in the corner of his eye; saw a figure moving quickly from the front of the car. It was Charlie and he was still armed. With a sneer spreading across his face, Charlie fired his last five rounds, each hitting their target. Jacob fell.

The bald man had made it to the top of the stairwell only to be confronted by Tal waiting patiently at the bottom. "Who are you? What do you want?" he demanded, raising his gun to meet Tal's.
"You have caused so much pain, hurt and misery" Said Tal "I'm here to see that..." Tal fired twice, both

shots penetrating the lungs of the bald man. As he slumped to the floor, Tal climbed the stairs and looked him in the eye. Unable to move and with life draining from him, the bald man succumbed to his fate, staring into the face of his killer. "I wanted to see remorse" Tal continued, "remorse for what you have inflicted on this world." He finished. Blood dripped from the thug's mouth whose face; turning an ashen shade, took on an expression of shame, like they always do when the realisation sets in that they are about to find out if hell is real. "There it is…" said Tal with a smile, watching until the final glimmer of life left the bald man's eyes.

He was on his back but still alive. He had taken five rounds to the chest and, despite the bullet proof vest, it had certainly hurt. He had been incapacitated for a brief second and knew he had to get to his feet. He rose to his knees just in time to see the butt of Charlie's pistol coming toward him at full force. It connected with the top of his head, dazing him but not enough for him not to be able to compute what was happening. If he was being struck with the gun, it must be empty. He also realised that his right hand was empty, he had dropped his knife.
"Shoot at me will you eh?!" Shouted Charlie, grabbing Jacob by the arms and hurling him toward the river. Jacob landed hard and attempted to stand up as Charlie closed the distance. Jacob got to his feet and managed to duck in time to avoid a haymaker, countering with a left hook to Charlie's kidney and right uppercut landing square under Charlie's jaw. It had rocked the big man but not stopped him. The two squared up, exchanging blows. Being hit by Charlie was like being hit by a sledgehammer. Jacob's best

chance was to stay in close; he had to eliminate Charlie's reach advantage. Bobbing and weaving he saw an opening; he used his Jab to distract Charlie and moved in again with a punishing right cross to the body. He heard Charlie exhale - his shot had landed but the big man was not swayed. "This needs to finish soon" Thought Jacob. From the first shot to this point, just over four and a half minutes had passed however it felt like an age. The police would be notified soon, if they hadn't been already, and their chances of success would be ruined. Charlie came at Jacob with another barrage "Shoot at me eh? You bastard!" he shouted forcing Jacob further back toward the embankment.

Jacob had to get Charlie down and quickly. He ducked low and delivered a brutal right hook to the inside of Charlie's left kneecap, it connected hard and he felt pain shoot through his clenched fist. Charlie let out a scream in pain and wobbled but regained his balance by leaning on Jacob. In a rage he raised his knee catching Jacob flush in the chest. It felt like he had been hit by a car. His legs gave way underneath him and he went limp as the air was forced from his lungs. Winded, he could feel his vision was closing in. Charlie raised another knee, this time hitting Jacob above the left eye and causing a deep cut. Two hammer fists to Jacob's back followed. Stunned and breathless, Jacob collapsed to the floor, blood covering his face. Charlie continued to deliver heavy kicks to Jacob who lay covering up as best he could. Breathing heavily, Charlie paused for a moment before he raised his leg ready to drive his heel through Jacobs head only to find himself suddenly being knocked sideways.

Tal crashed into Charlie with tremendous force and the two of them landed four feet below on the pavement of the lower tier. As Charlie attempted to stand but Tal swung his legs and caught him with a sweep sending him crashing down again. Tal manoeuvred himself above Charlie where he began throwing punches. Tal landed some powerful shots and bloodied Charlie's nose. Charlie, however, had weight and strength on his side; he managed to grab Tal's arms and pull him over to his right, gaining the dominant position. Tal covered up as best he could while Charlie rained blows upon him. Charlie again grabbed Tal's wrists and pulled his arms away from his face. Charlie drove his forehead down with all his might, the flat of his forehead landing flush on the bridge of Tal's nose. Blood erupted from his broken nose and his eyes misted as a second head butt connected. Tal couldn't see; he was on the verge of unconsciousness. Charlie placed his ginormous hand around Tal's neck, squeezing and pinning him down while delivering a volley of punches with his other hand. Tal was slipping away.

Jacob came round in time to see Charlie from the back, hunched over Tal like a bear over its prey, his left arm appeared to be pinning Tal down while he beat him with his right. Jacob tried to stand as a lightning bolt of white pain shot through his chest. His ribs were cracked, broken or both and he could only breathe in short shallow breaths. His eyes transfixed on Charlie, his will to help Tal driving him on. Clenching his teeth, he rolled on to his knees when he saw his knife.

Tal was numb; he couldn't feel anything anymore except for the motion of being struck. Things were moving in slow motion. Looking up he could just about see the dimly lit features and the blurred outline of his killer. He saw his attacker sit up and say something but couldn't make out what; he was losing his hearing as well as his sight. Gasping for air he could taste blood in his mouth. His arms lay outstretched to the side of him and he felt as though he were floating.

Charlie reached into his pocket and retrieved his trusty brass knuckles. He would put his fist through his bastard's skull for what he had done. He felt the satisfying weight of them as he raised his hand to strike the final blow.

Helpless, Tal watched from below. He saw something shiny with a shadow forming behind it. There was a black silhouette. It must be death, he thought here to meet me.

Charlie caught the figure in his peripheral vision, but it was too late. Death was there indeed but it was there for Charlie not Tal. Before he could react, Jacob threw his arms over Charlie's head and clasped his hands together around the handle of his knife. He shoved his right knee to the back of Charlie's head as he pulled the point of the knife back towards him. Charlie grasped desperately at Jacobs wrists struggling for control, but to little effect. As strong as he was, Jacob had the advantage. Charlie let out a shrill scream as the point of the blade slowly pierced his right eye. Jacob pulled harder until it came to rest in Charlie's brain where he twisted the handle 90 degrees for good measure.

Releasing his grip on the knife, Jacob stood back. Charlie stayed kneeling over Tal, head bent backward staring up toward the sky. Pain sparked through Jacob's chest as he placed an arm around Charlie's neck and dragged him backward to free Tal. As a pool of blood gathered at their feet.

With all his might, Jacob swung the bag of drugs and watched it disappear over the railing and fall to the river below, the effort making him cry out in pain. "We need to go, now!" said Jacob helping Tal up. The car was not far away. Leaning on Jacob for support, Tal could only wheeze and grunt as he limped along eyes half closed. Jacob wiped the blood from his nose on his sleeve and winced as the pain in his chest continued to seize him.

# CHAPTER 16

After a short struggle, the pair made it to the car. Jacob opened the rear door and helped Tal crawl inside. Tal lay across the back seats and went limp as he passed out. Jacob wasted no time in getting in the driver's side, starting the engine and pulling away slowly so not draw further attention to them.

He looked at his bloodied face in the rear-view mirror. It was a mess. Adrenaline helped numb most of the pain, however, and kept him going as he made his way towards the motorway to the north-west putting as many miles as he could between himself and the scene.

It was a long hard drive. He was exhausted but luckily the roads were not busy. Tal didn't move but made mumbling noises as he slipped in and out of consciousness. They had made it. They had survived. But only just. He wondered what his new employers would make of it, as deniable agents they could throw both Jacob and Tal to the wolves without a second thought. It made no sense to think about that now. Jacob concentrated on the road to take his mind off the Committee, off Charlie and the events of the night. He dared not think of Laura, when he did the wave of guilt that overcame him was worse than the pain in his chest. Concentrate on now, he thought, nothing but now, that is how you survive.

A little over three hours later Jacob pulled into the Manchester Royal infirmary. The building was an ugly mix of mirrored glass, red brick and grey concrete. He stopped the car right outside the accident and emergency doors. He rushed inside. "Help! Can somebody help please?" he shouted. The receptionist looked up; the waiting patients turned around and all visibly reacted to the bloody sight of him. "My friends in the car, he is unconscious. We got jumped about a mile away." False information but, if it came to it, they would have an alibi as to their whereabouts should they need it. Two nurses, one with a wheelchair, appeared from behind the counter and followed Jacob out to the car. "What happened?" asked one of them. "We were on our way to a concert, out of nowhere five guys just started laying into us" Jacob said. Enough truth to comply with their injuries but vague enough to not tie them to any specifics. To the hospital staff this would be any other weekend. After all, how many assaults are carried out in any given city over the weekend without being reported? He opened the rear door. "Mate!" he said being careful not to give away any name that might contradict any alias Tal might decide upon when awake. Tal murmured as the nurses helped him out of the car and into the wheelchair. "You go ahead; I'll get some stuff and follow you in" Jacob said, with no intention of doing so. As they wheeled Tal toward the entrance, their concentration on the task at hand, Jacob took his leave, and drove away unnoticed.

His ribs ached and his breathing was still shallow. He felt as though he had been at sea and he was beginning to get tunnel vision. Lights from passing cars dazzled him. He really needed to sleep. Eventually he rolled onto his driveway and parked next to his Defender. He slid out of the driver seat and staggered toward the front door. Reaching forward with a shaky bloody hand he inserted his key into the lock and pushed the door open, leaning on the door handle for support. Head down and clutching his ribs he fell through the door.

"Jacob, what the hell has happened?" shouted Laura rushing over from the sitting area. She had planned on surprising him on his return and had certainly done that. Jacob looked up to see a blurred outline. His heart filled at the sight of her as the world turned on its side and all went black.

# CHAPTER 17

Tal woke with a start. The last memory he had was being rocked by punches raining down on him. Confusion washed over him as he took in his surroundings. He was in a hospital bed, but he had no recollection how he had got there or even where in the country he was. "Where is Jacob?" he thought. "Is he ok, is he alive? What happened to Charlie? Did they succeed?" He sat motionless for a moment while his brain tried to piece things together. Looking around the sparsely furnished room there was little to help provide any answers. There was a small window, an empty chair and a console next to the bed. Tal took hold of the controller and pressed the assistance button in the hope that whoever came in would have some information.

Jacob could hear an unfamiliar repetitive beeping sound somewhere in the darkness. Why? He thought, why is that sound there? As the mental fog of his slumber cleared, he opened his eyes slowly. Everything was too bright. He raised a hand to shield his eyes and felt the slight restraint from an IV drip. Seeing him collapse into a bloody heap after arriving home, Laura had called for an ambulance. He was in a six-person ward with four other roommates. Two had visitors, one had the curtain closed and the remaining bed was empty. The clock said it was twenty-five to four. A sudden foul smell filled the room, betraying the patient behind the closed curtain. Jacob placed a hand on the mattress and attempted to sit up but was met with a sharp pain. He grimaced and clutched his chest. Reaching around he found the bed controller and raised himself slowly to get a better view of his surroundings. His forearms and right hand were bandaged, as was his head. He had Steri-strips applied to the cut above his left eye. There was an IV drip taped to his left hand. He still could not locate the source of the repetitive beep. He sat observing the room for a few moments and looking at the handiwork the medical staff had done while he was out. "Laura!" he thought, she had been at his house and now would want answers. He knew he would not have been able to keep this part of his life a secret from her; it was inevitable that she would find out, he just wished he could have told her first. After some time, a nurse appeared making the rounds. Seeing that Jacob was now awake he was eager to carry out some minor checks on the mystery patient. "Ah good to see you are awake Mr?" said the nurse. Avoiding giving a name, Jacob quickly countered "Great work you have done here" referring to his bandaging "what have we got exactly?" The nurse checked Jacob's responses making him follow the light from a torch with his eyes. "Well, you have a gash on your head, cuts to your forearms, a fractured right ulna and fractured metacarpal in your right hand. Extensive bruising to the torso, broken ribs and a severe cut above the left eye. Despite all that you will live"

Jacob smiled and said, "Well I must say you have done a magnificent job. When can I get out of here?" The nurse frowned and said "Unfortunately you are in no fit state to leave just yet; we will be keeping you in overnight. Best get comfortable and rest up."

Pretending not to be planning otherwise Jacob smiled and sat back. As he did so he caught a glimpse of Laura walking towards the entrance as the nurse went on to see the other patients in the room. He could see the concern on her face as she came in. "Jacob, thank god you're awake. What the hell happened?" She asked. Jacob stared at her unsure where to begin. He turned toward the nurse carrying out his rounds. "Nurse, could we get a wheelchair please?" he said. Reluctantly, the nurse finally gave way and Jacob was being wheeled by Laura toward the gardens. The automatic doors opened, and they were met with a cloud of cigarette smoke from patients and visitors crowded by the exit. Laura kept pushing the wheelchair with increasing anticipation as to what Jacob had to tell her. Her mind raced with endless possible explanations but the wait for the truth was becoming unbearable. At long last they arrived in an area with as much privacy as they could get. Wind blew through the trees and clouds formed and left overhead. "So, come on then." Said Laura "out with it. What happened?" her face had a serious yet concerned expression, her forehead was furrowed, she bit her bottom lip. Jacob could tell she was expecting bad news. "Do you remember our first date?" he began "You asked me to tell you about myself and I'd said I was a part time assassin or something like that." Laura looked at him quizzically and slowly said "Yes, I remember". He continued, "Well, in a way that was partially true, except I am part of a Government Agency. A secret agent, assassin, hitman call it what you like. I am part of an organisation that has now become a branch of MI6 that takes care of a certain undesirable, criminal element of society. The last task did not go as easily as others." He looked up at her to see her expression. She was bewildered and stared at him open mouthed, unsure whether to believe him. He wanted to console her in some way but could only sit in his wheelchair feeling redundant. She looked him in the eye narrowing hers and in a low but stern voice said, "You mean to tell me, that you expect me to believe…that you are some sort of fucking spy…that I am sleeping with a man paid to kill people when he is not selling paintings?" He could see the pain etched on her face. Perhaps he could have invented another story and gotten her to believe it but no. Against all odds he wanted to tell her the truth. He cared to much for her to spend any future together under a lie. She shook her head and turned away trying to make sense of what she had learned. Jacob thought about what he could add to maybe ease the revelation somehow, but he knew silence was his best ally now.

The wind blew, moving Laura's hair in the breeze. Jacob thought back to the night of the exhibition when they had sat on his couch, how relaxed and happy they had been. That memory now seemed tainted, looking at her now distance growing between them. Eventually, she turned to look at him. At first, she just stared as if trying to read him, trying to see the answers she sought in his eyes. Eventually she spoke. "Please, tell me you're kidding, whatever the truth is just tell me." Jacob swallowed, "That's the truth, there was never going to be an easy way to tell you. I am sorry Laura. People know there are people like me in the world; in this country doing what we do, it just happens to be that I am one of them. I can understand if that makes you uncomfortable. I also understand that you will probably need some time to process this but please know, I care for you Laura and I truly hope that I do not lose you because of this. If I could leave it behind, believe me I would do it in an instant, but I cannot, they have me Laura and I am not sure for how long." A moment of silence passed. "Your right." Laura said. "I need some time to think." She stood and placed a hand on his shoulder then walked away. Of all his injuries, none matched the pain he felt now.

He sat head bowed for some time. Unsure of what he could do to reassure Laura that it was just government work like being MP or a soldier, but he knew she needed time and eventually she would need answers, and there was only one person with that information. Despite the pain, Jacob managed to wheel himself to an area of payphones and dialled the number he memorised so long ago. The phone was answered by a male voice, "Committee cleaning services, how can I direct your call?" Jacob said, "This is Grey Wolf, get me Trafford now." After a moment, the voice replied, "Certainly sir, putting you through now." Things have changed quickly he thought as he waited for the call to be answered.

•••

Tal had been out for the count since Jacob had dropped him at the hospital. He had been hooked up to various monitoring devices and, although the doctors agreed that he was making good progress, they still had concerns. Despite his broken nose and fractured jaw, he also had swelling on the brain due to the trauma delivered by the hands of Charlie Hobbs. Amongst the staff he was known as 'Sleeping John Smith' as he had no ID on him nor had anyone called to enquire of his whereabouts that could possibly provide a name. Tal lay in a state of limbo. Through the darkness he began to see a light and something moving beyond it. He could hear something muffled but was unable to make it out. The light was coming closer, the sounds louder the images clearer. It was a figure, a large human figure. Just then Tal could see it as clear as day. He was under Charlie being hit; He saw Jacob approach Charlie from behind. He saw Jacob whip his arms over Charlie's head and drive a knife through his skull. At that point Tal saw a blinding white light. The flash subsided and his eyes began to focus. He found himself in a hospital room with his fists raised ready to fight.

# CHAPTER 18

Laura was sat in the window seat of the train with her headphone in. A book on modern art sat on the table in front of her and every time she glanced at it, she couldn't help but roll her eyes. She had bought it to understand Jacob's world a little more. Not that she had any intensions of becoming an expert, of course, but she wanted to know the difference between styles and artists to at least hold a conversation. It was his passion and she wanted to share that too. Now the book served as a simple reminder of her naivety. As she sat watching the blur of fields and trees rush by, she tried to recollect anything she could have missed that may have given him away as a hired killer. Sure, his house was huge, his car was expensive but his job selling art could easily explain that. After all Laura had experienced his talents first-hand. One of most frustrating things was that he had indeed told her but she brushed it off as anyone would but that was the issue. Why didn't she take him seriously for even just one second? After all, if all assassins looked like those portrayed in film, they would be noticed a mile away, but Jacob was kind, a gentleman, loving. How could he have this side to him and be ok with it? She knew she had been falling for him and she wasn't ready to walk away completely, but she needed time to think. She scanned the carriage and looked at the faces around her. They all looked so unhappy. Misery loves company she thought as she returned her gaze to the world passing by outside the window.

•••

"This is Trafford" said a stern female voice.

"Rebecca, this is Grey Wolf. The task was a success, the target eliminated, and the contraband destroyed."

"How and How?" She asked.

"TBI – traumatic brain injury. Fatal knife wound to the head. Cargo dumped in the Tyne river." He said.

"Fantastic and you and Rainbow, both ok and uncompromised?" She asked.

"Rainbow's current state unknown, he's in the Royal infirmary. I am in the North General. Injuries were sustained but we are clear, we left no traces." He said flatly. As though disappointed in the result.

"We knew it was high risk, had we had time we would have sent a whole task force. Next time I will make sure you have appropriate intel and time. I will send someone to check on Rainbow. Please believe me, I take care of my team and I do not think I would be so ruthless to send my people to certain death. This whole arrangement is built on trust, granted at this stage it is in the foundation stages but if I can trust you to carryout orders and keep off the radar, you can trust me to deliver you the best intel, weapons and support for the length of your career." Rebecca said.

After a pause Jacob spoke, "How long, may I ask, is this career, premature death aside?"

"Give me five years" She said, "Physical, mental checks will be carried out every five years to check your continued ability to perform and we review your employment on that basis." "And there is no way to resign and compensate before the five years?" He asked.

"No, I am afraid not" She replied, "Do your best and the time will fly by. Then, if we are satisfied, you can go on your merry way. Someone is on their way to check on Rainbow. You get some rest; we have more work to do and will be in touch soon." And with that she rang off.

Jacob stared at the handset before placing it back on the receiver. "Five years!" he thought before a voice interrupted his reverie "There you are! How did you manage to get all the way over here?" asked the nurse. "Anyway, doctors need to see you." He said wheeling Jacob through the corridors.

•••

A great smile crept across his face. From his hospice bed he had received a call from Rebecca Trafford thanking him again for the information he had supplied them, and to reassure him that his wife and daughter would be financially looked after in return for his assistance. In addition, there were absolutely no ties to his involvement nor anyone to carry out a revenge attack in any case. A great weight had been lifted from Terry's shoulder. A great weight of guilt and regret which he had been carrying all these years. He felt something he could only describe as absolution. The evening sunlight shone through the blinds making stripes of shadow across his bedding. Terry lay back placing his head on the pillow closed his eyes and let out a relaxing breath. Slowly his smile began to decrease until his face was expressionless. His work now complete, Terry Fletcher departed the world.

# CHAPTER 19

The pub was lively. It was modern and spacious so that, despite the clientele, Laura and Janet were able to have a conversation away from eavesdroppers. Sat in a secluded booth with a bottle of Sauvignon Blanc and two glasses between them, they began talking.

"So, Laura. Are you going to stop sulking and finally tell me what has happened, you have barely said a word since you arrived?"

Laura looked around the pub taking in the scene and took a sip of wine. "Something happened with Jacob. He has…He is…it's complicated."

Janet looked at her quizzically "A wife? Kids? Husband?" she asked eyes widening.

Laura put her hands to her face, "No he's not attached and it's not like that. It's that, he has a job alongside his business that I'm not entirely comfortable with." She was fidgeting with a beer matt and avoiding eye contact with her mother.

"Laura, if you want me to give you advice you need to be straight with me. Tell me what has happened."

Laura took a deep breath to steady herself. Leaning forward, she whispered, "He has some kind of involvement with the secret service." She looked around as if to check no one had heard her.

"And? So what?" Said Janet, "How many people in the UK work for the Government in some fashion?"

"Mum, I think he kills people!" Laura said, widening her eyes and making a shooting gesture with her hands.

Janet sat back with a thoughtful look on her face. "Hmmm, that is a difficult one to digest." Adding

"Do you know what sort of people it is he's sent to…deal with?"

Laura looked surprised "What do you mean, does it matter?"

Janet sat for a moment to choose her words, "If it is in the interests of national security, if it is in the interests of keeping people safe, if it is to remove undesirable creatures from the gene pool? Is it any different from a soldier being sent to combat terrorists? As you said it is part of an established Government organisation, so it is not as if he is a free roaming murderer. Did he tell you this information freely or did you find out somehow?"

"He came home covered in blood and passed out as soon as he got in the door. I got him to hospital. When I got there the next day, he told me."

"You see Laura; most men will not tell you what they are honestly thinking at the best of times. He did not try to lie to you or cover it up and I am sure there would be consequences for him if his employers knew he had told you."

Laura placed her hands on her head and said, "What are you saying mum?"

Janet lifted her glass, "Look, at the end of the day you were happy with him, from what I saw he would move heaven and earth for you. Just…" Janet let out a sigh "Just put this into perspective, you must be having second thoughts about leaving him, just give it some serious thought before you do anything rash."

Janet wondered if Jacob had any knowledge about her business with Gregory Malcolm. Surely, he must have investigated Laura and her family? If he was indeed part of the Secret Service. Janet felt a cold wave wash over her.

Laura was staring into space; she looked up at her mother for a moment and caught the pale look wash over her. "You ok mum?" She asked.

"Oh, yes I'm fine" She lied. "Come on, enough of the melancholy how's work?" she asked to change the subject and took a large drink.

# CHAPTER 20

The shop phone rang. "Knightsbridge" he said. "Is this Jacob" asked the female on the other end of the line. "Speaking" he said, "And who may I ask is this?"

There was a brief pause before she spoke, "It's Janet, Laura's mother, we met at the exhibit."

"Ah, Janet, yes I remember of course. How are you?" He asked surprised by the unexpected call.

"Laura has confided in me, about your…involvement with authority let's say."

"How is she?" asked Jacob.

Janet sighed "She's trying to get her head around it… If it is any consolation, I'm rooting for you two."

Jacob smiled slightly "That is very kind of you; please what can I do for you?"

"It's a little difficult, I'm sure Laura told you what happened to her father, my husband?"

"Yes, the hit and run, I'm sorry" he said.

"Thank you. The thing is, I'm aware the driver responsible recently…sorry this is difficult to put…"

Jacob understood saying "The Driver, Gregory Malcolm recently expired?"

Janet felt cold, he did know. Thoughts filed her head like a swarm of bees as she wondered if she would face prosecution for her involvement through the Committee or…what if he told Laura?

Finally, when she found her voice she said "Umm, am I going to be in any trouble?"

Jacob closed his eyes and took a breath then said "No, not at all. Not from the law and It is not my place to tell Laura."

"How did you know about it?" Asked Janet, "Have you been looking into us?"

"No" Said Jacob, "As fate would have it, I was tasked with your assignment."

Janet nearly dropped the phone. "Y-you? I" She took a breath. "David was everything to me" Janet said, "When that bastard got away with what he did. I, well, let us just say I found it incredibly difficult to go on. If it were not for the girls, who knows. Do you mind asking how…how did it happen? how did you do it?" Her voice trembled.

"Well, it was before I knew the connection between him and your family, had I known Laura before the event, well, I doubt I'd have passed on it but perhaps it would have been different. It was slow, he suffered before being asphyxiated."

Janet was silent for half a minute before saying "Do you think he knew; do you think he knew why?"

"Yes" said Jacob, "I have no doubt about that. The look in his eyes told me he had, the same as they always have is the look of panic, as the full extent of their wrongdoing becomes apparent and they realise there is no time for repentance."

"So why did you return the money?"

"I do not do this for monetary reward, I never have." Said Jacob.

"Thank you" Said Janet. "I will do my best for you where Laura is concerned."

"I appreciate that" Jacob replied. With that Janet rung off.

The shop had been busy since reopening. To aid his recovery Jacob had employed a young fine art graduate to help him. She was knowledgeable, eager and more than capable. She loved interacting with new customers and could talk art all day.

Jacob was almost back to full health apart from a niggling sting every now and again in his side when he moved suddenly. He had not heard from the Committee since the last conversation he had with Rebecca whilst in the hospital. Nor had he heard from Laura, though he thought of her often. Occasionally memories played through his mind like scenes from an old film. He missed her terribly. He often met Tal after work. Tal had been recovering well and taking it easy. It helped that following their last task they had both received substantial payment for their work. Since it was on official Government payroll, Jacob felt he could put most of it towards his retirement fund while donating ten percent to various charities. Tal was in the early stages of a relationship with Andrew, who he had bumped into in his building a while ago. The days came and went. Oh well, he supposed it was time to move on.

# CHAPTER 21

It was almost eight weeks since Tal and Jacob had completed their mission in Newcastle. There had been no word from the Committee, Rebecca or otherwise. Thankfully there had also been no interest from the police either, meaning no traces had been left. Jacob had been busy painting a new piece. His right hand was still healing so he was forced to take frequent breaks. Cramps would affect his grip of the paint brush. He set down his tools and picked up his cup of coffee. Taking time to observe the creation coming to life before him. He was distracted by a sudden knock at the door.

At the door, he was surprised to see Laura. She stood at the end of the steps biting her bottom lip as he knew she tended to do when nervous. Birds chirped in the trees and a car drove past.

"It's great to see you" Jacob said breaking the silence and doing his best not to be overcome by emotion and do or say something stupid.

"You look well" she said, "better than the last time I saw you at least." She looked at the ground and continued "How have you been?"

Jacob tilted his head to toward her and she raised her gaze to meet his eyes.

"I've been ok. Shops doing well, I have hired an assistant. Recovering well all things considered."

"I spoke to Tal recently" She said attempting a smile. "I didn't know he was wrapped up in this kind of thing as well?"

Jacob shifted his wait to his other leg.

"Tal has a soft spot for you, you know. Do you want to come in, so we can talk?"

"Yes" she said with a sad smile.

She had the most expressive eyes; Jacob could see the uncertainty. He knew this would be a make-or-break conversation and he knew he would fight harder than he had against Charlie to keep her.

Once inside she looked around remembering how comfortable she had been the last few times she had been there.

It now felt strange the way she acted like a first-time guest.

"Please take a seat; can I get you some coffee?" He asked.

"Coffee would be great thanks" she said, walking past the painting and taking a seat in the living room. "I see you're painting again?" she asked.

"Yes, I've been dabbling, slightly hindered by the hand at the minute but giving it a go." He said. Coffees made, he set the cups down on the lounge table and sat at a ninety-degree angle to her. The last time they had been so close, now it was like they were strangers all over again.

"Tal told me what happened, He is very thankful you saved his life." She said.

"The man you killed, he was, a criminal?" She asked. Jacob looked at the floor and said, "He was an animal. Had we not intervened countless more lives would have been ruined for his personal gain. Drugs, human trafficking, abuse. You name it he had a hand in it. He was a cancer. A plague. The world is better off." He reached for his cup and sipped his coffee. Laura studied him to see if she could learn anything from his body language. He was still not giving anything away.

"Have you ever killed someone who didn't deserve it?"

She asked.

"No, each were guilty beyond doubt. Including Gregory Malcolm" he said looking her in the eye.

Laura's eyes widened. Her mouth fell open in shock.

"Him? What did you do?" she asked.

"I removed him from the world. I was assigned a task; he was the target. It was before I knew about your father but as you already know, Gregory was another person hell bent on destroying innocent lives for his own gain."

Laura exhaled processing this new revelation and swept her hair from her face, tears forming in her eyes. "Jacob, I'm not sure what to do. I know that staying with you means that I will have to either accept this, which might take a bit of time or pretend as though it is not real. I'm not sure I can fool myself." A tear fell to her cheek.

Jacob reached a hand over to her, Laura took it and squeezed. Jacob moved closer so he was sitting beside her.

"I have to give them five years. After that I am free. In that time, I may get a hundred tasks, I may get none. It may just be surveillance, following people, it could be more, I don't know. What you need to remember is that this is about making our country safer."

She looked up at him eyes filled with tears biting her bottom lip again. "Of all the people, I have to fall for a bloody assassin, spy whatever the hell you are." She said smiling. Jacob wiped the tear from her cheek. She raised her head to meet his gaze. He leant forward and kissed her. As she raised her hands to his face, he put his arms around her. It felt so good to have her back.

# CHAPTER 22

It had been over six months since the incident in Newcastle. Laura and Jacob sat outside of a beautiful restaurant in Corfu town. The building that lined the wide pavement had fantastic archways offering shade to patrons who sat on wrought Iron cushioned chairs and looked out over the park. It was nearing 2pm and the weather was sublime. They had been there almost two weeks staying in an apartment and having a fantastic time.

As they sat drinking Chilled wine and cold beer they talked about the house, about Tal and Andrew, Knightsbridge and her upcoming exhibition in London. Jacob checked his watch, "Any moment now" he said. "It's terribly exciting, what do you think she's going to say?" she asked wide eyed with intrigue. "Ah here she is" Jacob said as Rebecca Trafford approached them. They stood to greet her, "Rebecca, good to see you" said Jacob, "This is Laura…"
 "Very pleased to finally meet you both in person, so sorry it took so long but I had to make sure the circumstances were right." Rebecca said.
They sat down and Jacob motioned to the waiter. "Iced Coffee, please" said Rebecca. The waiter nodded and went to complete the order.
"I can now confirm their intention is to kidnap a certain diplomat's daughter in an aim to exhort leverage. We believe this to be the orders of David Windermere."
David Windermere?" asked Jacob. Rebecca replied "He's an arms dealer who we believe to have

connections to political and diplomatic assassinations, both foreign and domestic. David has a perverse political agenda and an underground network of loyal supporters who believe the days of the old British empire should be restored."

"What else do we know?" Asked Jacob, "date, time and location?"

"Yes Jacob, all in good time. All intelligence on this matter is being collated at Committee headquarters. A detailed report will be available for you in due course."

Laura sat back and sipped her wine, watching, listening intently. The real-life plots were as gripping as the stuff they peddled on TV.

Jacob gave her a smile, she smiled back. The waiter returned with Rebecca's iced coffee, placing it down and saying "Yamas!" then went about his business conversing with the other waiters.

"So, the question is…" Rebecca asked leaning forward; looking back and forth between Jacob and Laura, "Is this something that we can count on your assistance with?"

Jacob looked at Laura and smiled again. Laura held his gaze and smiled back and replied "You certainly can…"

## About the author

Ben Belcher is a writer, a musician and author of the new novel *Exposure.*

In his professional career he works as a Facilities and Contracts Manager. Ben has spent the last few years honing his craft, absorbing himself in the crime and thriller world to enable him to bring his characters to life with credibility and integrity.

*Exposure* is his debut work and is the first instalment of *The Redemption Series*.

Ben was born in Canada. He grew up travelling extensively with his family, living in many countries including four years in South Africa. He experienced many different cultures and traditions. He is highly skilled at target shooting and is a 2nd dan in the Japanese martial art of Iaido.
Ben currently lives in Manchester with his wife their son and the family cat. He is a lifelong film nerd and a devoted fan of the Japanese actor Toshiro Mifune. Those that know him would say he has a wickedly dry sense of humour.

Printed in Great Britain
by Amazon

59111490R00085